SWORDS OF THE SEA

Kingdom of Frendilar Series

Book 1

TIMOTHY RIVARD

PAGE PUBLISHING, INC.
New York, NY

First originally published by Page Publishing, Inc. 2015

ISBN 978-1-68139-692-7 (pbk)
ISBN 978-1-68139-693-4 (digital)

Printed in the United States of America

CONTENTS

PROLOGUE

The kingdom of Frendilar had thrived for years and most recently had withstood its longest patch of peace. For nearly a century, war had existed only in stories, battle existed only in sport, and armies had existed only for show and tradition. The reason for this peace could be found stationary, as far north as it was possible to travel. A large tower stood erect looking down on the northern coast. Sharp and dangerous rocks surrounded the tower to the north, as well as the sea, and when the tide was in, such as now, the waves crashed into that natural rock wall that made up the cliff face that the tower was built on top of. This natural cliff face, though massive in height, looked tame in comparison to the height of the tower that had been built upon it. Nearly forty stories in height and nearly wider than any castle in Frendilar, it was an amazing feat and would be marveled at if the entirety of the kingdom didn't know that it had been built with magic anyway.

It shone across the small town that surrounded it. Built entirely of white marble stone, it had been erected to remind the kingdom of what the mages stood for—peace. And although the mages had succeeded in bringing about the longest stretch of peace the kingdom had ever seen, the tower was seen more as a symbol of power than a symbol of peace. The mages didn't rule the kingdom directly, but they did keep those who did in check.

At the very top of the tower, the fortieth floor was a room like any other in the entire building. It was the largest room in the entire tower, circular like the tower itself, and was used by no more than ten mages at any given time. As the large yellow sun hung highest in the sky, that large circular room held host to two mages. The first, a young man dressed in a long white mage robe. The robe itself distinguished that he was a mage; the color distinguished his status. This man was calm and light footed, almost bouncing on his feet. He had long, flowing silver hair and an almost childish smile upon his young-adult face.

Dracut, the other man, was no older than the silver-haired youth, but he was built so differently. His fighting stance was solid and unmoving, and his overly large muscles held two large black maces above his head. While the silver-haired man bounced continuously on the balls of his feet, Dracut, with his short black hair, didn't even blink. More of a statue, he was almost teasing his opponent, appearing unready to battle when he was indeed more ready than he could possibly be. He stared across the large, empty room at his opponent; those dark-gray eyes stared back. Neither Dracut nor his opponent seemed capable of blinking as they bore into each other, both attempting to read the other's actions before any true movement occurred. Dracut's heart began to pound, his adrenaline pumping. He gripped his two heavy and deadly maces in his hands, sweat pouring over his fingertips. The maces weighed greatly on his muscles as gravity pulled the heavy masses, but Dracut had long ago gained the muscular endurance to hold those maces high for a long time without ever growing weary.

His opponent held his two rusty old swords lightly in his hands, which were unlike the heavy masses of Dracut's dual maces. His opponent's stance was light, quick, and balanced; his gray eyes were staring hard at Dracut, his cleanly shaven face shining brightly from the small bit of sunlight shining in through the nearest window. Dracut ignored the reflecting light, ignored the magnificent mane of silver hair his opponent had tied back. Dracut was always jealous of that natural silver hair, for when his short black hair went white, it would be a symbol of old while he showed off that elegant silver hair as a symbol of his youth. Dracut moved his focus back to his opponent, but his opponent had already seen his change in concentration.

It happened quickly, his opponent's amazing speed and agility pushing him forward across the room so fast that if Dracut had indeed blinked at that time, he would have already lost the fight; but Dracut was no novice to fighting this opponent, and both his heavy maces were lifted in perfect timing to parry the incoming swords. With the speed of a trained warrior, he quickly reversed direction of his right mace, its momentum picking up quickly as his strength gave it speed. His opponent ducked below the swing and backed up as Dracut quickly pulled the mace back again with little effort.

In came those dual swords again, almost instantly, and Dracut almost missed a low parry with his left mace as his head dodged the high jab of the other sword. His right mace came back quickly, pushing his opponent back and to the side but never connecting. The sound of dull metal echoed through the empty room as two maces connected with two swords again in a deafening double parry.

Dracut could feel himself breathing heavily as he yet again managed to pull his right mace up to parry a high cut from his opponent's swords, but his left mace could not swing out in an offensive move as one sword quickly dropped low to be parried again by Dracut's left mace. His opponent's strength was his speed, a speed Dracut could not match. Only his years of training with the heavy maces were keeping those rusted blades away from his skin, but he knew, too, that his opponent's weapons were a lot lighter than his. Time was not his ally.

His opponent knew, too, that Dracut would tire first, and Dracut could easily see that his opponent's attacks were aimed at keeping him moving his maces defensively, refusing to give him time to attack. Few of his opponent's thrusts or slashes were even aimed at a vital point on his body, but he could not let the blades pass, and thus, yet again, he moved his maces down and up to parry incoming swords, swords that moved with grace and agility. Dracut was no novice to battle, and to most men and women, his skills with his maces would have proven fatal already—but his opponent was better, had always been better.

The swords came in high and low again. Dracut moved to the side, dodging both in a hope to get an offensive swing off for the first time in minutes; his maces swung out, but they found nothing to connect with for his opponent had foreseen the move and had sidestepped as well, the swords coming in at an impossible angle. Dracut barely managed to get his left mace to swing back toward his opponent, knocking the closest sword away, its momentum pushing his opponent to the side and keeping the second blade from connecting with his neck.

The battle turned quickly in his favor as Dracut noticed the sword he had hit land on the ground a few feet away from his opponent. He didn't wait to give his opponent a chance to recover the blade, quickly swinging both maces ahead, but his opponent was quick and parried both swings with his one remaining blade. Dracut did not let up, however, both maces swinging constantly. With each great swing, he expected to hear the sound of one of his maces connecting with his opponent.Every time, he heard the distinct sound of metal on metal as his opponent's speed and defensive movements kept him parrying and dodging each and every swing of the fast and deadly maces.

Dracut took a chance, swinging one mace in an overhead downward swing and forcing his opponent to dodge by sidestepping to the right, and swinging his other mace horizontally to connect with the sidestepping man in front of him; but his opponent dodged the downward swing, and his single sword parried the horizontal mace. Then his opponent spun, coming around the parry and behind him with speed Dracut could not expect to match. In a defensive move, Dracut spun, both maces spinning with him, one high, one low.

His opponent was crouched low, ducking below the high-swung mace, his sword parrying the low-swinging mace. It was then Dracut recognized his brutal mistake for his opponent lunged forward then, his second sword aimed directly at his stomach. Dracut could not expect to get his high mace down fast enough to parry that jab, and his other mace was connected with his opponent's other blade. Dracut had lost sight of the dropped sword, his opponent had not. Dracut let out a sigh of defeat and exhaustion as the sword collided with the magical force field around him, sending an electrical sting through his body. He dropped his maces to the ground and looked at his best friend who was smiling, always smiling.

———●◆✕◆●———

"You're getting quicker," Jaxxal said as he leaned on the window of the sparring room. He seemed much shorter now that he had stopped bouncing on the balls of his feet. He peered out the window, that young smile still shining brightly on his face. Sweat was dripping down his face from his mane of silvery hair that was no longer neatly pulled back after a long afternoon of sparring with his best friend.

Dracut did not respond as he hung from the ceiling in the middle of the room, focused on a small metal box attached to the ceiling. His best friend, Jaxxal, stood looking out the window on the farthest edge of the large circular room while Dracut continued to pull on different-colored strings—or were they strings? They didn't react to his pulls like strings, but they reacted like beams of light. One arm was strapped in to a large leather rope, and the work he was doing was working on the strength in his arm just as much as working out his brain on the magical device he was playing with.

"Sooner or later, you may actually beat me," Jaxxal's voice was almost pleading, asking for a response, trying to remind his friend that that day would come.

Dracut did smile but, yet again, said nothing as he fought with a white beam of light that refused to bend in the direction he was bidding it to. He was not upset that he had lost; he had expected it,He had never been able to win in a duel with his friend. Jaxxal was the only fighter in the entire mage tower he could not defeat in battle, and he often reminded himself he was glad his deadliest opponent was his best friend and not his enemy. But even then, he could not deny that his greatest desire was to be the best, to surpass his friend in his combat efficiency.

"It's going to be a beautiful night," Jaxxal added, again pleading his friend to respond with words as he watched the sun set below the ocean's horizon. Jaxxal never got sick of the view of the sea from the top-floor sparring room and often wondered what could be out there, beyond the kingdom of Frendilar.

Dracut smiled. "Another day at its end," he said. "Another beautiful day to follow.Another day with no word and nothing to do but be reminded again and again how much better you are than me." He dropped down from the ceiling, stretching the arm that had been holding him up, and frowning at the white beam of light that was now bent in an almost spiral shape.

Jaxxal's mouth opened to spill forth a denial of his friend's words, but the smile on Dracut's face reminded him that he was not depressed or worried by what he said. There was a measure of excitement and anxiety in both their hearts. The kingdom of Frendilar, the kingdom all mages fought to protect day after day, seemed a small, insignificant piece of their future at that moment in time. Both of them had pledged their lives to defend the peace in the kingdom. They were two of the ten Tailles of the mages.

In the language of the gods, *Taille* meant "elite," and that's exactly what the Tailles of the mages were. They were the elite, the best of hand-to-hand combat among all the mages and could be both the strongest allies and the worst of enemies. There were always ten Tailles—exactly ten. Neither Jaxxal or Dracut could have explained why that was the case or why the top two floors of the tower were only accessible by the ten Tailles; that was just how it had been for nearly a century. Six of the Tailles were out on missions in the kingdom; four remained contained in the Tower of Council,two on bed rest, Jaxxal and Dracut waiting patiently beside them for that something more important to both of them than the peace of the kingdom. And although patience is one of the most important parts of their warrior training, both Jaxxal and Dracut had little patience remaining these days.

Few words were spoken between the two friends as they watched the sun set together.By the time the sun had vanished, the two friends traded places. Jaxxal lifted himself with magic to the ceiling and grabbed a hold of the leather strap in the ceiling and began examining the strange shape the white beam of light had spiraled into. Dracut moved to a different window and looked down onto the small town below the tower that consisted of the homes of the mages. By that time, most of the tower and town would be asleep;Dracut expected only a few could possibly still be awake at this time so early in the fall. He pictured many older students awake, reading books by candlelight, overly preparing for an exam the next day. He wondered if the next Taille mage could be among them.

Jaxxal dropped from the ceiling and nodded to Dracut, approving the shape of the white beam of light in the metal box of colors. Both Dracut and Jaxxal began to wonder if they should be joining the mass by going to sleep in their quarters on the floor below when the large door to the Taille training room burst open. Both trained warriors didn't react in the slightest to the sudden sound that filled the room. The large wooden door had rocketed forward, obviously having been opened by magic. Jaxxal only then realized they had left it locked.

An older female mage came into the room. Her light-blue robes were a clear indication that she was from the healer's guild, a group of mages who practiced and learned the technique of healing and life itself.

She didn't need to speak a word; her simple nod told both Dracut and Jaxxal what they wanted to hear. Both sprinted for the door, and the healer simply, but quickly, moved to the sideto let the two Taille mages escape through the open door.

Down a full flight of tower stairs the two leaped, and a magical residue remained in the air behind them, assuring onlookers that magic alone had allowed the two to land on their feet without the slightest bit of pain. Down flight after flight, they ran and jumped until they reached the twentieth floor. They stopped their unnecessary sprint as they came to the door of the healers guild, reminding themselves who they were, and instead of busting down the door in order to enter quickly, the two friends walked calmly through the doors into the Healers Ward.

The two did not walk far before finding their objective. Two beds were side by side, and in them were the other two Taille mages remaining in the tower. There in those beds lay their wives. Jaxxal's wife, Juhni, was smiling brightly although tears were rolling down her face. Her long blonde hair glistened from the bright magical ball of light floating above her. She was wrapped in a light-blue gown and was holding a newborn baby, wrapped tightly in a light blue blanket.

Lying in the bed beside her was Dracut's wife, Vixxen. Her raven hair was a mess and was lost somewhere under her, and Jaxxal couldn't help but realize how long she had truly let it grow now that he was seeing it down for the first time in ages. She, too, was dressed in a light-blue gown, but the newborn child she held was wrapped in a pink blanket, and Jaxxal couldn't help but smile at his wife and her best friend. He couldn't help but smile at his best friend as well before each of them walked to his wife's side and were both given the chance to hold their newborn children.

Neither Dracut nor Jaxxal heard the healer enter the room, and for the first time in a long time, both flinched as she spoke to them. "Born at the same time," said the old healer. She smiled, but Jaxxal and Dracut had stopped smiling. Her presence reminded them that this moment would be short lived. "At the exact same time," she added, obviously unaware of the change of atmosphere she had brought into the room—or was it just that she was so used to the reaction. Dracut turned and looked at Jaxxal, and he was returning the same look. Mages did not believe in coincidence.

"The council has decided to agree with your request and will secure your children in the same city," the healer again said. "Their fatesare obviously intertwined." The healer left the room then, giving the four parents a chance to say hello to their children and possibly, more importantly, the chance for them to say good-bye. For the child of a mage would not receive his or her magical abilities until they turned fourteen years of age, and the tower and town had been designed and built with all sorts of magical protections; it would be too dangerous for the child of a mage to grow up there. And it had become clear early on that the son or daughter of a mage was unsafe in the real world when there were people looking for power in anyway it can exist. Mages learned all about the history of the first attempts to keep children in nearby towns with human families. Kidnappings had become extremely common, and so for his or her own safety, the child of a mage was secretly secured in a human family in a random town. It had worked for years; kidnappings ceased completely, but parents had to continue their lives for over fourteen years before seeing their children again—but it was necessary.

"Good-bye, Mistirie," Dracut said, patting the bald head of his daughter.

"Hello," Jaxxal said staring at his son. "Hello, Shaydix."

All four parents were smiling and crying. Some tears were of joy, some of sadness. In that moment, it would not have been possible for any mage to know that in just two years' time, the entire way of life in Frendilar would be threatened by an unknown source of power.

1

A Long Time at Sea

The waves of the ocean crashed into the side of the large ship, and although the wave was two times the height of any human, the ship barely rocked as it pushed against its side. The largest ship of the entire fleet, the *Hailstorm* sailed in front, leading over three hundred ships, most holding over a hundred men and women warriors from the Xile Tribe. Their leader, Deerskyn, stood at the bow of the *Hailstorm*, looking out over the ocean, restless and eager for battle.

Just over seven feet in height, Deerskyn towered over all his people, and his muscular arms were twice the size of any man he'd ever met. Those of the Xile were all warriors, men and women both, and Deerskyn was their leader by the simple fact that he was indeed the most powerful, the largest, and, most importantly, the most cunning. His long dark hair waved behind him as a gush of wind crossed the deck of the boat, and the smell of the sea attacked his nostrils again. There was little to smile about these days for Deerskyn missed land greatly.

"If we do not find land soon, it will be the end of all of us," Deerskyn said in both a no-purpose tone and an accusatory one. Behind him on the bow, the sound of metal on metal rang out against the sound of the ocean waves as two long metal spears collided. Deerskyn's only son, Fortilian, was breathing deeply as he backed away from his sparring partner and looked upon his father in a questioning way.

Fortilian was certainly his father's child. Just under seventeen years, Fortilian stood eye to eye with his father and could stand well in a fight against his father, but there was something more to the power that was Deerskyn, a presence itself that his son did not have—a presence that provoked both fear and respect from all his people. His son would no doubt grow still, and perhaps in time, he'd develop that same presence; but for now, he himself turned his glare into a smile although Deerskyn did not turn around to see it.

"You expect another fight will come?" Fortilian asked, hinting at the many one-on-one battles that had occurred among their warriors traveling on the ship. He walked over to his father and joined him looking out upon the sea, his spear still in his left hand as he used his right hand to pat down his unruly, scraggly black hair. It had been much worse out here on the sea than at any time before on land, and during his sparring matches against Magicot, it took on a mind of its own.

Deerskyn didn't quickly respond to his son, and while he thought about his words, he did smile at the sight of his son, still so young to be able to worry about simple matters such as his hair. Deerskyn was not so lucky, and he thought back to the truth of his son's words. He knew it was simply the way of his people, always at battle, always at war with one another. He'd led them out because of the word of Magicot, his trusted shaman and advisor. He'd been told of a land far to the west, in the direction of the setting sun, where he'd be able to find the war his people needed, a war for more land than they'd ever known on their puny island, a war with people not of their own. It was something Deerskyn felt his people truly needed, but as his son so simply reminded him, of late, many had become restless in the wait for battle and had begun taking it out on one another despite his constant warnings that this war they were heading to would be more difficult with every loss of a warrior.

"Their need for battle outweighs even their fear of you," Fortilian said, pulling his father's mind from his own thoughts. His son had stopped playing with his spear, and his teenage smile was gone as he looked into his father's eyes. Deerskyn lost his smile as well then.Perhaps it was about time he remind them why he was their leader. He had worried that any sign of physical ramifications might be counterproductive since he was bringing them across the ocean in hopes of giving them a common enemy to fight, an enemy that would not be oneanother.

"I spoke clear when I stated no fighting was to be brought upon any aboard, that we'd need every able fighter ready when we land. I wish it was as simple as speaking strong, but I'm thinking it may take a bit more than that if we are to stand any chance."

"Many speak now about never finding this land we seek," Fortilian stated as he turned around and headed back to his sparring match. Deerskyn turned around, putting the sea to his back. "Keep an eye open,Dad.They may be looking for a new leader before long."

Deerskyn shrugged; he had dealt with plenty of would-be leaders attempting to take his place in the past, and he was still leading them. He would not be so easily defeated, but he could not deny that even he was beginning to grow weary of the journey. Their supplies were nearly at half of what they had been when they first sailed out from their home, and if they did not turn around soon, they'd never make it back with their current supplies. Deerskyn watched as his son quickly loosed into well-timed swings and parries, and the shorter and weaker warrior that was Magicot kept up with him, matching every swing and every dodge.

Magicot knew how to fight, although being a shaman, the only magic-using member of the Xile tribe, did of course give him a mighty advantage. Either way, it made a father happy to see his teenage son fight with such control. Magicot was decked with jewels, and it never made sense to any other member of the tribe why he coveted such useless treasures, but Deerskyn believed that each one of those sparkling gems that the young man decked himself out in had magical properties, possibly giving him more defense than any of the basic leather armor the rest of the tribe wore into battle.

Deerskyn smiled as his son miraculously dodged an incoming fireball and managed to stay standing as Magicot released a strong gust of wind in his direction. Magicot was smiling as well and nodding in approval. The training was greatly important because it was likely their new opponents would be using such tricks against them as well.

They ended their sparring then, and both the young shaman—with his leather outfit bearing jewels of many colorsand hisyouthful face—and his sweaty but happy, youthful son joined him at the edge of the boat.Both looked out, searching for land, but there was still a decently heavy fog settled upon the ocean that morning.

"What about the other ships?" Fortilian asked. "We cannot doubt fighting is happening on all of the ships in the fleet." Deerskyn could do nothing but nod in agreement for he had been thinking the same thing. Each boat had been given a captain, and Deerskyn knew better than anyone that by now, some of those captains had changed and blood had been spilled.

"We can only hope that the captains your father appointed are keeping order on their ships. Although it may be about time I travel around and check out how the other ships are doing." Magicot said all this and didn't wait for a response from his leader before jumping over the side of the ship. Father and son soon saw the shaman riding a magical wave in the direction of the closest ship, and they both watched as he vanished into the fog. They didn't get a chance to begin a private conversation for a sound from below distracted them seconds after Magicot vanished from sight. The sound of splintering wood found home to his ears, and a frown found its way to his lips.

"Another one," his son stated simply. Deerskyn knew, however, that this problem was far from simple. He heard the shouting, some cheering, and some screams in protest; he knew most were staying quiet though, waiting to see how the fight ended.

"Come," he said to his son as he began to walk to the door in the deck that led below to where the battle, or fight, was taking place. "It's time I put a permanent stop to all this."

If the shouts from below hadn't been so loud, and if the sound of fist to bone had not been filling the ears of those below, they'd have known for sure that their leader was crossing the deck. Deerskyn did not use the slightest bit of stealth in his walk across the deck of the ship and down the stairs into the large, open living quarters below deck for he knew he did not have to. He looked into the rooms, and he was not at all pleased to see that he was correct in his expectations, even if he had been certain.

A man nearly ten full years over his own, but not yet old enough to sport gray hair, was smiling as he took another full swing into the chest of a boy no older than Fortilian. The boy took the punch, wincing in pain for it was far from the first he'd received, but he did nothing to retaliate and took another punch in the face for not fighting back. Blood splattered along the fist of the older warrior and the newly growing blond beard of the younger boy gained a few more bloody spots.

"Dad," Fortilian said, helplessly looking to his father. Deerskyn understood fully for the boy was choosing not to fight back because of his own orders. Another swing collided with the boy's elbow as he attempted to block it away, and although the boy was above six feet in height and full of muscle, he was indeed feeling the pain of every hit.

"Stop this at once!" Deerskyn shouted down into the room below. His voice was louder than every other voice below deck, and some would have sworn it shook the boat itself. The shouting stopped immediately, and the only sound that followed Deerskyn's own voice was the sound of the waves outside the ship. Deerskyn finished his journey down the stairs and into the room, trying to decide how best to handle the situation below.

It had not been the first fight he'd stopped thus far as his bloodthirsty people sat awaiting battle, trapped on the open sea. However, it was high time he made a clear message, but he wasn't sure how best to go about doing it, and he was taking his time making his way over to the older fighter. It wouldn't matter what he'd decided though, for as he passed by the young boy that had been taking the beating, he noticed then that the older man was attempting to deliver a message. The boy Deerskyn passed by was none other than Manatin, the son of Deerskyn's best friend. Rage took the place of calm and cunningleadership. There was no order or plan to his actions then, just pure anger.

"My orders were quite clear," Deerskyn stated angrily. The usually calm and levelheaded leader suddenly reached the older warrior, and if the Xile Tribe had believed in respecting their elders, he would have still had none to give.

The old warrior shrugged. "Every boy could use a bit o' toughening up. He'll take a better beating once the war has begun." It was a rehearsed response, and one Deerskyn had heard all too often in the last few weeks at sea. He had expected the response, but this time, it didn't even register in his head. He wasn't about to make an argument, wasn't about to remind them why this pointless fighting needed to stop. He was done talking.

Perhaps the older warrior recognized the different response for he quickly changed tactics. "It shall not happen again, my king," the old man added. Deerskyn still didn't hear a word the man said, nor would it have mattered if he had been sane enough to pay attention. He reached forward as the man bowed slightly in a fake apology that did nothing to calm the rage boiling inside Deerskyn's blood at that moment.

The entire crowd seemed to stand still as Deerskyn wrapped his large fingers around the wrist of the man. Although older than himself, the warrior was not weak by any standards except, perhaps, if Deerskyn himself set those standards. There was a reason Deerskyn was leader, and he was about to remind them all what that reason was.

The sound of cracking bone brought a greater silence to the already quite silent room; it seemed all of his people had suddenly stopped breathing, and the only movement was the fall of the older man—the fall to his knees, finally begging and apologizing for real. Deerskyn did not hear his cries and just held tight to that broken wrist, continuing to crush the bones beneath his deathly grip.

"My orders were clear," he repeated firmly to the man. The man nodded fast and repeatedly, wishing his king would release the grip on his now broken wrist, but Deerskyn's rage was far from abated.

"Dad," his son's voice sounded far away at that time, and he knew it was begging him to return from his anger. "We need every one of our warriors for the coming war."

Deerskyn smiled, and the man's face showed a bit of relief, expecting his leader to release his grip; but Deerskyn continued to tighten his grip on the man's wrist, crushing the bones into many pieces. "That I cannot argue," Deerskyn said, loud enough for every man and woman in the room to hear. "But anyone unwilling to follow my orders is not one of my warriors." And before the look of shock and surprise appeared on the old man's face, he found himself flying across the under deck and smashing hard into the wall of the *Hailstorm*. Two distinctly different cracking sounds echoed through the ship, that of bone on wood and that of wood splintering. Water rushed in around the now dead warrior, but not a person moved.

"Quickly now," Deerskyn ordered with every last bit of rage that remained in him. "Fix the ship and toss the soon decaying corpse over the side of the ship." He smiled then, finally regaining his calm, and added heartily, "I wish not to sink, nor to spend the next ten nights smelling the death of this filth."

He turned to his son and Manatin then, and all three were smiling; Manatin, perhaps, more than all three of them—a smile Deerskyn would not have believed could get wider. He was proven wrong by a sudden scream from above.

Deerskyn could barely make out the one word that was being yelled. It was only the repetition of the word that finally got through to him.

"Land," Deerskyn repeated.

"Land," said Fortilian.

Shouts of "Land!" filled the entire room at that time. They'd have their war soon enough.

2

AT A DISTANCE

The sky was still bright from the evening sun as it began to set behind the forest trees, casting a beautiful orange and red glow across the clouds in the sky. Below those clouds stood a small but well-built town known as Duerken. Duerken stood alone in the farthest northeast corner of the entire continent of Frendilar. Surrounded on three sides by the ocean and by the forest to the west, it was a lonely town, unable to rely on nearby towns for help constantly. Perhaps that was why it was considered a trader's paradise. The citizens of Duerken relied upon the goods that traders brought in to town, and luckily, Duerken had a great gem to trade with for the fishermen of the coastal town were adept at not only catching fish but fished up pearls as well.

The only travelers were not always traders for the coastal town boasted a powerful connection to the sea, and many traveled just to see its sight and revel in the beauty of the town. Few places in Frendilar compared to the town of Duerken besides, perhaps, the castles of the kings or the mage tower itself. Most common among its visitors were its traders; both legal and illegal traders came to Duerken in hopesof selling off their wares for the pearls they fished up. The citizens of Duerken were unaware of how truly valuable pearls were for the ocean surrounding Duerken was the only place where the waters were calm and shallow enough to fish for them. However, so far from other villages was the town that its citizens often could not get everything they needed, and so it came down to the traders to get it to them. More often than not, the valuables of a trader would fetch a much higher price in the ocean-side town, a known fact that Hugheny Dastal often took advantage of.

Hugheny sat with his legs crossed on a small set of stairs leading into one of the many pubs that lined the center square. Trader's Center was what they called the large circular setup of buildings that created the circular center of the town, lined by pubs, inns, rest areas, and even some craft shops. In the center of the circle was a large wooden circular platform that rose high above the ground; the platform resembled a stage so well that it was not possible it could be anything else. Outside the buildings were all sorts of trader's carts, many of them selling much more necessary goods than Hugheny carried or cared to carry. Hugheny was not a normal trader for he dealt with the black market, selling stolen goods and magical items that were normally confiscated by kings and mages.

Hugheny normally wore a simple black hooded traveler's cloak so as to blend in, but Duerken was a colorful place, and black would make him stand out, so he was currently dressed from head to toe in a bright-yellow traveler's cloak he'd won in a game of cards many years before. It shone brightly, and although it might be hard to believe, he actually blended in better with the crowd in such a garment. His blond hair was long and curly, puffing out and giving him an almost lion-like appearance. If only he'd ever been able to grow a beard, he might have appeared as old as he was.But Hugheny had always looked younger than he was, and although he had been trading in the black market for nearly twenty years, he found that his youthful appearance made fools mistake him for a fool.

Hugheny was, luckily, a patient man for many traders had begun packing up as the sun continued to set behind the trees, and his contact had still not shown up to collect. He watched as two small boys climbed on top of the stage-like platform, swinging wooden swords at one another. Not a member of the community seemed to care, and Hugheny found himself feeling jealous of the children who had not a care in the world.

Hugheny squinted against the assaulting glare of the sun and leaned back more against the stone wall behind him so as to force his eyes within the shadow of a building. Although Hugheny had lived nearly forty years, nearly two-thirds that of which he was expected to live, he did not expect to ever have children of his own; and as he watched the two boys playing, he wondered if it had ever been in the cards for a man of his secret talents. His sparkling blue eyes gave his youthful face an appearance of innocence, and his smile to an older woman, who passed by carrying what appeared to be a large bag of wool, kept his presence there attention-free. Perhaps his height of barely five feet added to that youthful, almost childlike, appearance he held. He folded his long yellow traveling cloak around his body at the approach of a man but half his age, who seemed to be the only one taking any interest in Hugheny.

The man was dressed in a dark-blue soldier's uniform, and patched onto both shoulders was a bright-yellow star, the symbol of a captain; Hugheny recognized that proud and strong stride he took as he walked directly in his direction. His short brown hair, he knew, too, was also a part of his uniform because most men did not bother to cut their hair that short except those who joined the Duerken army.

"You haven't been causing any problems today, I hope," the man said, speaking directly to Hugheny.

Hugheny instinctively thought of the many hidden knives he carried in different secret places under his cloak. He didn't expect to need them, but it was a defensive instinct to remind himself where they all were. A mischievous smile spread across his face as he spoke to the captain, "Always up to something, I am. But no, I'm afraid I've caused no trouble this day."

The captain gave Hugheny a half smile and shrugged. "Been a bit boring around here, could be using a good show." Hugheny did not miss his subtle gesture in the direction of the center stage.

He also understood perfectly the indication the captain was making. Most often, the stage was used for public whippings, tortures, and hangings, although the latter was not too common in the last hundred years.

"You'll find I've calmly kept to myself, I'm afraid." It was not the truth, of course, and the weight of eight gold coins in his pocket reminded him he'd made out all right that day.

The man shook his head. "That will not do." He moved closer and took a seat beside Hugheny, almost appearing to be scolding him. He leaned over and whispered, "Did ye get the blade?"

The smug merchant nodded his head, and when he was sure not a soul was looking in their direction, he slid a small dagger out from under his cloak. A beautiful weapon was that dagger, obviously made for show more than for any form of fighting for the dagger held nearly ten bright-green gems in its handle, each believed to be enchanted with some form of magical spell. The silver blade was what gave the blade away for it did not reflect the light as one would expect; it instead absorbed it, creating a shadow on the blade wherever light touched directly.

"The price is still the same," Hugheny said as he shook the dagger out in front of the young captain, teasing the man who he knew had coveted such a blade for years.

"Worth every bit of it," the man said. Hugheny handed over the dagger then and watched as the muscular captain walked away, his long captain's sword swinging in rhythm at his side as he walked away with that same prideful stride.

The captain stopped and turned back for one more look at Hugheny soon after the sun shone directly on him, almost like a spotlight. Hugheny had to remind himself how important it was to stay on the good side of Jahkan Yute, for it was never smart to get on the bad side of a captain of the guard in any town, not to mention one of their elite guards, but Jahkan displayed a pride with both his stare and his walk, an air of confidence that Hugheny did not doubt was well earned.

The sun yet again shifted into his eyes then, blinding him momentarily. At first, he could not discern how the sunlight had already moved so much as to reach his eyes, but as he found the shadows again, he noticed the sun had not moved to blind him, but instead had been reflected—reflected off the bright white coat of a beautiful horse, a horse of such beauty even one who had never visited the town of Duerken before would have known the man riding it to be of importance. Hugheny disappeared into the shadows of the building; he was not well liked by the lord of Duerken. The lord of the town had stopped to speak with Jahkan then, and Hugheny recognized the worry in the lord's face.

So with the knowledge of having twenty days of guard-free trading by Jahkan's promise, and a very expensive stolen dagger out of his possession, Hugheny disappeared into the shadows of the coming evening and vanished quickly out of view of the lord of Duerken.

Lortael, the lord of Duerken, was an old man, nearing the last of his years on the land, and he'd all but given up hiding his age from the citizens of his town. He'd been a good lord, and not one of his citizens believed him to be anything but his usual self; and although nearing the end of his days, the old lord was far from dead at that time. His bald head was covered by the metal helmet he wore, scratched from front to back, a reminder to many of how strong a fighter he had been in his youth. He sat upon his magnificent horse with an aura of confidence that not a man or woman would deny him. A frown painted his face that day though for word had begun to spread that something large was headed their way on the sea.

"Boats?" the youngest of his captains asked, walking toward a wall on the street, Lortael and his horse following him at a slow trot.

"Large boats," the old lord stated. "Larger than anything I'd ever be seeing, and no boat that size could harbor anything friendly."

"We can't be knowing that for sure," Jahkan said, leaning against a wall and sliding both his hands behind his back in a comfortable position, specifically to be sure the dagger he'd just purchased stayed well hidden in his back pocket till a proper sheath could be made for it.

"Don't ye doubt it for a minute," his lord stated again. Obviously, he'd already decided that the boats the mages had warned them about and that had been spotted earlier that day could not possibly come to Frendilar in peace.

"What would you have me do then?" Jahkan said, choosing not to concede to his lord, but neither did he choose to argue. His hands were beginning to sweat, and he knew the longer he stood there talking, the longer his lord would have to discern that he was hiding something.

"Speak to the other captains," Lortael said. "And seek me out a messenger, the fastest you can find."

"To seek the aid of the mages?" It wasn't a real question for Jahkan already knew himself to be right. It was a predictable response to a possible war, especially one that would cripple nearly three generations of peace. His lord only nodded in response, his eyes looking to the sea.

"Perhaps it is best we learn a bit more before sending a messenger. I'd be hard-pressed to find two fastest messengers one after the other." Jahkan, who was about to smile, shied away instead for his sarcasm was apparently not welcome to the ears of his lord.

"Find me a messenger and bid him to inform the mages that they were correct and that the boats have been spotted. Have him inform them that they definitely appear to be heading directly in the direction of our town, and I expect them to send help immediately. We could be looking at war in less than three days."

"One," Jahkan corrected him. "It will take even the fastest messenger two days to travel so far east to the Council Tower."

"Two then," his lord stated, shrugging as he stared out toward the ocean again. "Send the messenger to the academy instead of the tower. They can then carry the message to the council by magic."

"And thus, you see why you are the lord and I serve you," Jahkan said with a mock bow. A smile crossed Lortael's face then, showing that he did indeed catch on to Jahkan's game but seemed to enjoy the flattery nonetheless.

The horse and Lortael quickly departed those streets, leaving the sweating Jahkan to stare in disbelief toward the ocean. He realized if he did not get a glimpse of these ships now before darkness fell, he'd have to wait till morning, and he wished to see them before he found a messenger.

Quickly, the young captain sprinted down the street. So fast was his stride and so important his destination he did not notice the many looks of the traders and buyers in the streets, who seemed suddenly very interested in Jahkan, nor did he recognize the shadowy figure that followed him along the walls of the street.

Faster he ran as he came closer and closer to the edge of the town. Many, he noticed, were already standing out of their houses and looking out across the sea, past the harbor, and across the darkening ocean sky. Jahkan came to an abrupt stop as he saw the large masses far out in the distance. There could be no mistaking their shape even at such a distance; they were certainly boats, at least a dozen that he could see, probably more. His lord had told him nothing good would come of it. As he stared out at the boats and the dark clouds that seemed to follow them, Jahkan did not think he could disagree.

———◆◆◆◆◆———

Hugheny stared out across the ocean with the rest of the citizens standing near the flat ground that many often used to side up to the ocean line. The entire city's small fishing boats seemed to be pulling back in and weighing anchor at the sight of the oncoming large boats. Hugheny guessed then, and he was not the first to do so, that the city of Duerken had no more than three days before those boats would be landing upon their shore.

The sky itself seemed to tell the tale of the coming ships. A bolt of lightning far out at sea flashed across the sky and lit up some of the traveling boats. The demon ships were too far out to discern anything specific about them, but Hugheny didn't doubt for a second that *demon ships* was certainly the appropriate term for the coming boats.

Hugheny looked over to Jahkan then and was not surprised by the fear that showed clearly on the young captain's face. It was a fear that mirrored everyone in attendance. The dagger Jahkan had so desired had given the young thief twenty days of freedom in Duerken. It seemed he would not be getting his full payment after all.

THE CROSSING

The sun had already begun to dip below the horizon's edge, and the tide on the southernmost tip of Frendilar was in as deep as it could get. The waves rose unnaturally high and crashed back down with the force and anger that was the fury of the sea itself. The rocky beach that made up the southern tip was void of life for there was not a more dangerous shoreline in all of Frendilar. But on this rare occasion, one woman was tempting fate trying to cross the deadly Forbidden Sea.

The waves crashed around Juhni's tiny wooden rowboat, but she managed to keep the boat afloat with determination. Her tiny rowboat rose fast and then fell fast, splashing into the water as another large wave rushed below it. She pushed in one direction with her right oar, steering the boat just past a large sharp rock under the water. She had reached the most dangerous part of the passing as the rocks she now had to avoid were invisible. The knowledge of how to survive traveling the Forbidden Sea had been passed down to her when she became a Taille. She had hoped—prayed, even—that she would never have to make the journey for even with the knowledge she had been given, the Forbidden Sea could be deadly. Juhni only knew of one human who had ever successfully made the journey, her master and teacher.

Another large wave lifted the rowboat in the air, this time dropping the boat so fast it floated above the water for a second, long enough to crash back into it. Juhni's long, shiny blonde hair dipped into the water as she lost her balance, and only because of her sheer determination did Juhni manage to right herself in time to steer clear of another invisible rock below the water's surface. With a quick reaction, her left oar managed to make contact with solid rock and push off it, maneuvering the boat far enough to the right to avoid the crash of an oncoming wave. This quick response managed to keep her afloat for the time being.

Juhni took a second to breathe as the waters calmed down. This was not the first time she'd thought the sea had relaxed though, and she could not let her guard down again. Her memory began quickly remembering the timing and location of the invisible rocks below, keeping the boat on the proper path. The sun was quickly vanishing, washing the ocean with a light that only dusk could bring. The sun should have brought Juhni a bit of comfort, the light giving way to a slightly less dangerous journey. But instead of peace, it brought her fear for time was running thin, and she had a long way to go still. The boats the council had foreseen coming to Frendilar could have arrived already, perhaps visible to the villagers and guardsmen of Duerken. If the boats were hostile, a battle would be coming, and she was running short of time.

There was no guarantee that the Seachurns would help the humans or the mages, but if the seers were right and the boats were indeed as numerous as reported, then they would need all the help they could get if it came to war. As the keeper of the path of the Forbidden Sea, it was Juhni's responsibility to make the dangerous journey to the Seachurns' inhabited island in hopes of gaining an audience with the queen. It had been a while since the mages had had any contact with the Seachurns, and Juhni felt it was all for nothing. She would much rather be with her husband, Jaxxal, talking about their son, Shaydix, and preparing to fight alongside him. She would even have preferred to travel to the Fury Isles with her husband, but the Seachurns would never welcome a human male, and her husband had a responsibility all his own.

As if sensing her reduced concentration, the sea roared angrily again, and dark clouds appeared like fog around her. The light from the sun diminished, the waves grew larger and stronger, and the ocean breeze became cold and biting. Juhni's right oar made contact with a rock, the wooden oar splintered upon it, and shards of it cut deeply into her right arm. She quickly tossed the broken oar into the water, grabbed the spare from the bottom of the boat, and steered the boat clear of another incoming rock. She focused hard, allowing her instincts to kick in as her teacher had taught her.

Seachurns navigate the waters with a magic given to them by their god, their creator. You will need to navigate the ocean waves and rocks by instinct and knowledge alone.

The two oars struck a rhythm as Juhni focused on her knowledge of the path she'd been taught. She continued to dodge invisible rocks and managed to keep the boat afloat despite the growing waves. The winds picked up, and her hair swirled around her head, restricting her sight even more than the dark fog had managed to do. She quickly took a second to place the white hood of her cloak over her head. She stopped for a moment to tuck her hair into it and then pushed off a rock with her left oar. It was a hard push meant to push her over the oncoming wave, but instead, it pushed her fully into it. With a large crash and splintered wood, Juhni found herself entirely submerged below the water's surface, the strength of the waves pushing her back toward the shore and into an invisible rock she'd already steered past.

With concentration and a sheer determination to survive, Juhni forced the water to turn around her. It stopped pushing against her and instead surrounded her, the current creating a circle around her and encompassing her within a protective watery cocoon. She then forced the water out from the cocoon, creating an air bubble around her. Juhni gasped for breath and pulled a small, hollow metallic rod from within her cloak. The rod just barely fit in her hand, no longer than the handle of a sword and no thicker either. It was the tool of a mage, that which allowed them to channel their magic, to strengthen it. No two rods were the same, molded from different materials, engraved with different runes, and were even of slightly different sizes. The rod was a mage's most valuable tool, as well as a combat mage's most trusted weapon.

Juhni knew what she needed to do now that her boat had been destroyed, but before she was able to focus her magic into her runic rod, her protective bubble hit the point of a rock and popped. The ocean water began to rush around her again. Her lungs stopped receiving oxygen as her breathing ceased. The rod began to glow a tinted blue, and the water itself began to form below her, taking on the shape of a boat and pushing her to the water's surface. By the time her head broke into the oxygen-filled air, the water that had pushed her to the surface had solidified into a rowboat of ice. The boat was floating peacefully above the ocean that had almost swallowed her whole.

Juhni was on all fours within the boat, her head tilted down as she coughed up the seawater that had begun forcing its way into her lungs. She banged her fists upon the boat of ice, coughing, breathing, and then coughing again. She had never felt so close to death, and her husband's face clouded her thoughts. The first cry of her son filled her head. It took her some time to realize the sound of waves was missing, and it was no illusion that the last rays of sun were shining around her again.

She sat up as soon as her body would allow her, and she let her gaze search the ocean around her. There was not a sign anywhere that the ocean had so recently attempted to take her life from her. The black fog had dissipated entirely, the wind had stopped, and the waves were nonexistent. The ocean was at peace, and she happily felt herself at peace, glad that the first step of her journey was complete. She looked up to the heavens and thanked her god, Totailon, for giving her the courage to take the journey. And then with a bow, she thanked Trillo, the god of the sea, for granting her passage through the goddess's home.

Juhni knew, of course, that her journey was not complete, but the most dangerous part was over. The Forbidden Sea was there to prevent anyone from passing within range of the Seachurns' home, and once passed, there was only one other obstacle to overcome—the ocean itself. The ocean would not allow a human to pass a certain point for it protected the island.

With a deep breath, Juhni's heart came to a rhythm of calmness. She lifted her runic rod, and with light concentration, her magic filled the rod and then grew outward as water, forming the shape of an oar made entirely of water. Water was the element that made up almost all of Juhni's weapons. An oar was not necessarily a weapon, but its creation was similar and thus did not need to be separately conjured like her boat. Once the oar was complete, Juhni wasted no time in rowing forward, remembering her responsibility, remembering her goal.

Juhni knew it wouldn't take long until she found what she was looking for next in her journey. With every stroke of the oar, she flinched, expecting the boat to stop abruptly—not from any invisible rock, but from an invisible wall. The sun had vanished entirely below the horizon before the boat crashed into the Seachurns' invisible barrier. It was an invisible wall that kept anyone from finishing the journey to the islands above the water. Since Seachurns could change their feet and legs into long, scaly tail fins and breathe through hidden gills, they had no need to travel above the water. Juhni was not a Seachurn, but her master had taught her a spell that would allow her to make the trek to the Fury Isles. Juhni was but the only mage to have ever been taught the spell.

With legs crossed, she held her oar of water sideways in her hands and closed her eyes and focused. She listened to the sounds around her. The wind was whistling in her ear as it blew calmly by her. She could almost see the ocean creatures making splashes in the ocean as they broke the barrier of water and air. She listened to the waves as they rocked the boat. She focused on the slight rocking of her boat as the ocean waves, although barely as high as a fingertip, rocked the block of ice back and forth. She allowed all the peaceful sounds to block out the pain in her right arm, and soon her oar changed shape again, protruding from the back end with water as well. The head of the oar curved and contorted into the shape of a trident. The length of such a weapon, a spear, a staff, or in Juhni's case, a trident, gave balance to the mage's concentration of magic. It was with weapons of length and balance such as these that allowed a mage to truly bring out all that their magic had to offer.

Juhni had used spells to transform herself into different objects and appearances before, but as she focused upon this spell, she didn't feel the usual uncomfortable feeling of changing. The transformation this time was sudden and instant. She didn't even feel the change till she had already toppled over the side of the boat, tailfin and all. As her head splashed below the waters, she noticed the gills on the side of her neck and recognized that she now had the ability to breathe underwater. She had succeeded in transforming into a Seachurn.

The spell was only temporary, but it would last long enough so that she could swim to the Fury Isles, which was the home of the Seachurns. Her goal was in reach, but time was not to waste. Juhni removed her white mage cloak for it would only slow her down under the water. She watched as the symbol of her elite status among the mages floated slowly to the bottom of the ocean floor. The mage cloak would mean nothing to the Seachurns, and she expected they wouldn't recognize that the white of the cloak meant she was a Taille. As she realized she was unaware of how the Seachurns would react to her visit, it became apparent the more dangerous part of her journey may be yet to come.

4

THE ACADEMY OF KNOWLEDGE

Night passed quickly for Hugheny as he and his light-brown horse traveled through the eastern forest to the eastern mage academy. As the sun began to rise above the trees, the path Hugheny traveled brightened, and its end began to seem nearer. The horse felt as if it picked up pace, and it seemed that just as he began to wonder if he'd ever reach his destination, it came into sight. The rest of the path was downhill, and as the horse ran, he pressed it on faster. The dust of the dirt road grew larger behind him, and the air began to pass by harder and quicker, and then he pushed the horse even harder. The horse was tired, Hugheny was tired, and a full night's ride left them both hungry, but his goal was in sight. A tall stone building that towered above the trees themselves was his destination. The academy was surrounded by open land despite it being in the middle of one of the thickest forests in Northern Frendilar. The large black fence that protected and surrounded it was a sight to behold.

Hugheny had traveled to the Academy of Knowledge only once before, but this had appeared to be more times than most of the available messengers in Duerken, and Hugheny had been certain he could reach it fastest. He had been paid well to carry the message for the guards, and since the majority of his earnings were that of a nonhonest trade, it felt right to earn a bit of gold in an honest way.

It felt especially good considering the importance of the matter. His mind floated to that of his message now as the academy began to grow ahead of him. The building itself was fashioned with perfect cuts of stone and was full of carvings with so much detail that only a hundred crafters could have built it—or in this case, one mage crafter.

Standing among the trees on opposite sides of the forest path were two mage guards dressed in pitch-black cloaks. The golden *M* on the sleeve gave away that the cloaks belonged to mages, and Hugheny almost didn't see them standing there. With their hoods on and covered by the shadows of the trees, they almost skated by unseen; but the moment he was in range of them, they stepped out onto the road, and his horse halted immediately as swords of flames erupted in their hands. Hugheny felt himself almost flung from the horse's back, and his stomach suddenly felt as though it was spinning. It was the first time in hours that he felt glad to have eaten very little recently.

"Who are you?" one guard asked.

"And state your business at the academy," the other said immediately after.

Hugheny was still attempting not to vomit air and found it very difficult to answer the guards' questions quickly. His lack of response did not appear to be a problem though, for although the questions were asked in haste, it appeared they were prepared to wait forever for a response from Hugheny.

"I am a messenger for the lord of Duerken," Hugheny finally managed to state. "I bring urgent news that could disrupt the peace in Frendilar, and it must be transmitted to the council as soon as is possible."

The swords of flame were distinguished then, and both guards turned to look toward the academy gates. Hugheny wondered if that meant he was free to carry on, but before he got the chance to move, he was reminded why so many feared magic. The ground beneath the mages suddenly turned to lava, and out of them quickly climbed two magical horses. These magically summoned horses had manes that were on fire and tails that sparked flames when they swayed. If it weren't for the flames in their eyes, Hugheny could appreciate such beautiful horses with coats of a lovely charcoal. But he'd be lying if he said he was not intimidated by the beasts and the men who rode upon them.

"You will follow us," one guard said with a stern look.

"If you stray from the path or appear to fall behind too much, you will be considered a threat," the other continued. And then immediately, their fiery stallions began to gallop toward the academy gates, and Hugheny felt himself pushing his horse to follow quickly out of instinct and fear.

The mages in front of him kept a very steady pace toward the academy, thankfully, making it easy to steer clear of bringing any suspicions upon him. They seemed focused on the path, but somehow, Hugheny knew they were just as focused on him and his whereabouts, possibly even on the nervous vibes he knew were emanating from his body language like alarm bells. The mages continued to prevent Hugheny from calming his nerves as they pulled out their flaming swords again as they reached the gates. They raised them high above their heads, and Hugheny could feel the heat pulsing out from them; the brightness forced him to look for something else to focus his eyes on, but all that he found were the large black gates.

The gates were made of solid stone with the head of a dragon carved directly in the middle. The dragon head did nothing to reduce his fears; in fact, as the eyes began to glow a bright red, his fear increased greatly. Then, with what sounded like what he'd always predicted a dragon's roar to sound like, the stone gate split in two by fire and began to open inward. The mages extinguished their swords again and moved to the sides of the gate, signaling Hugheny to enter.

Hugheny did as he was instructed but kept his horse at a friendly trot through the stone gate. For a second, he thought it would close mightily behind him; but as he passed it, the only sound that came in contact with his ears was a friendly greeting.

"I do hope our guards did not frighten you. They do quite enjoy scaring our guests." A man in a dark-brown robe stood in front of him, and with the hood of the robe off and a bright smile greeting Hugheny, his fears were abolished completely. "My name is Labyrint."

Hugheny recognized the importance of the brown robe Labyrint wore, and before even greeting the man, said, "I'm surprised a member of the council would be here at an outward academy."

"All of our academies are watched over by a council member," Labyrint said. "It keeps the students, teachers, and guests feeling comfortable and safe within our walls."

Hugheny wished he'd known that the last time he'd been at the academy. If he'd known a council member was present, he'd never have stolen the dagger from within its walls. Luckily, he did not appear to be recognized. "I have come from Duerken with a message of great urgency. It appears a dozen or more large boats are heading straight for the town, and to be honest, sir, they do not appear at all friendly."

"We don't expect them to be," Labyrint stated simply. "Come inside, and we can discuss what you've seen and what we know. I expect your trip has left you hungry." Hugheny could not disagree, and he let a teenage boy tend to his horse as he was led into the academy and to an empty room full of tables and chairs. An older lady with many wrinkles entered the room. She had steady hands despite her age, and Hugheny recognized the light-blue cloak that she wore to distinguish her as a healer. She brought them both plates of wild fruits from the forest, and Hugheny waved off manners to fill his empty stomach.

"Now," Labyrint said as he nibbled on a tiny red berry, "how many boats did you say there were?"

"A dozen, at least," Hugheny said after swallowing that which he'd been chewing. "I expect there to be more."

"A lot more." Labyrint shook his head then and stared at the stone ceiling above. Hugheny followed his gaze, but he could not see anything upon the ceiling to look at. "The seers at the tower have seen the coming of these boats a few days before today. Hundreds of these boats, possibly holding hundreds of men on them. The problem is, we know nothing beyond that. We do not expect the intentions of these men to be of a friendly variety, but we have no way of being certain."

Hugheny was taken aback. "Hundreds?"

Labyrint only nodded in response. "If it comes to war, we have already taken every measure we could. Messages have been sent to all neighboring villages. Luckily, a few of them had ambassadors there who could be contacted by magic. The Tailles have all been alerted, but we expect only one will be able to arrive in time for the start of any fighting."

"Only one Taille?" Hugheny could not hide his disappointment. "The most powerful mages and warriors in Frendilar, and only one will be able to arrive for the start of a war?"

"Start of a war with thousands of men," Labyrint reminded him. "The Tailles that had been at the tower at the time were sent out to seek help from the Seachurns and the Woodnips. And we had to send Dracut to the Dark Mountains to see if the Ashens may have had any information."

"The Ashens have been extinct for years," Hugheny said almost angrily.

"Yes, but their information did not go with them. Knowledge could be the deciding factor between saving lives and losing them."

Hugheny had no reason to doubt the wisdom of the council no matter how crazy their ideas seemed to be. "I should return quickly then to inform Duerken. They should be as prepared as possible."

"I would hope you could wait a little bit," Labyrint stated. "I'd like to introduce two mages." As if on cue, the two guards that had led Hugheny into the academy entered the room. The guards had their hoods off, and they were both smiling and laughing with one another as they entered. It contrasted completely with Hugheny's first interaction with them. If he hadn't met them before, he would be completely unafraid of the two combat mages who wielded swords of fire. Also, with their hoods down, Hugheny was able to recognize how similar in appearance the two were. They were young, probably hadn't even seen twenty winters; and if their hair had been cut in similar lengths, he'd not have a way to tell them apart.

"Twins," Labyrint said, stating that which Hugheny had been thinking.

"They are the only ones I've ever seen wearing black mage robes," Hugheny said in response, pointing out something a little less obvious.

"That is because they are the only combat mages in the north prior to the Council Tower itself. They are stationed to guard the students who study healing, history, and knowledge. They are the only combat mages who could possibly arrive in time to help from the beginning of this invasion. So I will be having them tag along with you."

Hugheny smiled then.Although he preferred to travel alone, he was glad that there would be some early help from the mages. Even if he was not prepared to fight in the battle himself, he did have friends, or the closest thing he had to friends, residing in Duerken.

"Don't ask if they talk either," Labyrint said, standing up and sending the two guards to get ready. "They may seem stern and focused now, but if John here starts talking, you'll never get him to shut up."

The guard with long blond hair smiled at that. "I know. I've tried," he said. The one with the shorter hair responded by punching his brother in the shoulder.

"I have to keep talking," John said, "or Jine here might actually get a word in."

Hugheny suddenly wished he'd be traveling back alone. He'd been around twins before, but never twins who wielded swords of fire and rode horses that the god of hate himself would envy. It seemed like a dangerous pairing.

5

TWO TAILLES

A branch of the utmost thinnest found itself caught on a cloak of white as a woman of beauty crept quietly through the brush. She had barely seen more than twenty-five years pass, and yet she looked even younger than that. Her short ebony hair was hidden entirely within her white hood and, with the lightest tug the branch, found itself free of her cloak without having the slightest chance to make the tiniest of sounds.

Vixxen knelt at the edge of a clearing in the eastern forest, not but a few minutes from the trail she'd been traveling. She knew the trees were watching her and recognized her existence in their forest, thanks to the many conversations she'd had with Jaxxal about the Woodnips; but she was not heading deeper into the forest, and thus felt safe from the Woodnips. Someone or something else, however, had been camping near her the night before, and with the possibility of a coming war, she was, sadly, a bit paranoid.

Her nostrils flared as she again took in the smell of ashes,clearly indicating a nearby fire that had only recently been put out. Someone had been camping in that clearing over the night. She peered through and was not surprised that the clearing was empty besides the remaining ashes of a recent fire. Whoever had been camping there had only recently left. She blamed her paranoia on the onset of battle as she was traveling to the town of Duerken. But it did not sit well with her that someone, anyone, could be so close to her without her knowing who it might be.

It did, however, calm her down to find easy-to-follow tracks, and this could only mean a few things: they weren't trying to hide, they were lazy, or, the best possibility, they were really just that stupid. Vixxen found it easy to follow the tracks through the forest's edge quietly. Whoever it was she was following was just slightly taller and larger than she herself was, and the path they had taken through the woods had been cleared for her.

Vixxen soon found herself back on the path she had previously been following. It suddenly occurred to her that whoever she was currently following was probably heading in the same direction she was. This was most likely the sign of them being an ally, possibly a messenger or reinforcements sent to Duerken from the eastern academy. She looked in both directions on the stone-like path, but there was no indication among the stone that anyone had recently traveled upon it. Her instincts immediately kicked in as she reached for her runic rod inside her cloak, a weapon no mage was ever without.

A voice spoke then, and her name traveled to her on the back of a friendly and familiar voice. She turned around to see Isaic exiting the forest. Isaic was indeed larger than she was, but not by much; he only stood two inches above her in size, and he was the smallest of the male Tailles. His pitch-black hair was offset by his forest-green eyes, and as he exited the forest, she noticed his skin was changing colors—from a dark greenish shade to a much darker but normal skin pigment.

"Only you could hide so well in the forest's edge," Vixxen said matter-of-factly. "The Woodnips themselves would have trouble finding you."

"The Woodnips can speak with the trees," Isaic said in a hushed tone, "and I may be able to use magic to blend in with the forest colors, but the trees don't see as we do." Vixxen laughed, but only for a moment. She was surprised to see him so close to Duerken. When she'd left the Council Tower, Isaic had been in the southern kingdom attending the wedding of his sister.

"I did not expect your travel from the southern kingdom to be so quick," Vixxen said. "Did your sister drive you away from her wedding?"

"Although it wouldn't surprise anyone if that was the case, no," Isaic said. There was a sarcastic and annoyed sound to his voice. "If you must know, my sister postponed the wedding due to some issues with where they intended to live. My father is giving her a large amount of land to use since I am obviously never going to need it, but she is not entirely sure she wants to stay in the southern kingdom. She wants to travel like her little brother and check out some ocean-side towns."

"Does that mean your dad is blaming you?"

Isaic chuckled. "I didn't stick around to find out."

"So you were already on your way back to the tower when the council's message reached you?" Vixxen knew it to be the truth as she spoke it, and she had to admit she was glad not to be the only Taille that would be in Duerken when the boats arrived.

"Hundreds of large boats," Isaic said. "How could that possibly be friendly? Do they know anything about it at all?"

"Afraid not, it's why I'm the only one headed to Duerken."

"Only one," Isaic was obviously surprised by the news. "I could have sworn, when I left, at least Dracut was at the tower with you."

Vixxen nodded as her mind wandered to her husband. She was headed to a battlefront, and she was more worried about him. The Shadow Mountains hadn't been visited by a mage since the end of the Mage Wars, and although both the dark mages and the Ashens were extinct, the dark energies that surrounded the place could be treacherous to any man.

"Dracut was sent to see if he could learn anything from the old libraries of the dark mages."

"I'm surprised they'd send Dracut—no offense intended, but Jaxxal would be a much better choice."

45

"Perhaps, and I'd not mind it be someone besides my husband. But Jaxxal is the only one the Woodnips would ever give an audience to."

"They are looking for help from the Woodnips?"

"And the Seachurns as well." Vixxen looked down the path then. She didn't know how long they had, but she had recognized the urgency in the council's eyes when they met. If this was war, it wasn't going to be quick or easy without help.

"Sounds like we are expecting war," Isaic stated simply and let out a deep sigh. "We better get moving then. A couple of mages may be needed to help calm the townspeople. There isn't a soul old enough to have borne witness to the last war."

"I'm not entirely sure what we are expected to do. We are human, so training in combat is always a part of our society, but we don't have the faintest clue as to who our enemies are, let alone what they are capable of."

"I think I'm more worried about what exactly it is they, whoever they are, may want from us."

Conversation between the two mages came to a close then as both mages pulled their runic rods out from under their cloaks. Their eyes closed at nearly the same time, and in seconds, a wind began to blow quickly around them. The earth shook below their feet as the nose of a horse protruded from the ground and another poked its way out of a nearby tree.

A charcoal-black horse climbed out of the ground, and a horse whose entire body matched the color of the tree bark walked calmly out of a large tree overlooking the stone path. Both horses snorted, and from the nostrils of the black horse, smoke erupted into the air. The mages looked at each other as they mounted their magical horses.

"I'm not sure I'm ready for a war," Vixxen said as the horses began to trot forward along the path.

"It's what we're trained for," Isaic said.

"Trained for combat and battle, but not even those who trained us have any experience in war."

"I believe you just found a downside of peace," Isaic laughed, but Vixxen's nerves held her stomach tight. She could only think of her two-year-old daughter, safe in some town, somewhere. She could only hope she'd live to see her again.

The two Tailles picked up the pace of their horses, pushing them forward, aware they did not know how much time they had till they would be needed in Duerken. At their new pace, it was difficult to have a conversation, but Isaic continued to be confused by the council's decisions.

"I wasn't actually in the council when they made the decision. Only Jaxxal was in attendance," Vixxen said as she enjoyed the passing air created by the increased trot of their horses.

"Jaxxal would, I expect, have been the one pushing hardest not to separate the Tailles."

"Of course." Vixxen shook her head even though Isaic was ahead of her and thereforewas unable to see her do so. "But they were very stubborn. Jaxxal thinks they are worried it could be the prophesized return of the dark mages."

"I suppose that would explain the need for help," Isaic stated. "If it is, then we surely haven't been trained to fight a second mage war." Vixxen didn't say a war. As she thought about how few combat-trained mages still existed, she realized they were not prepared to fight any war.

"So main goal, I suspect, is to evacuate the civilians?"

Vixxen nodded, and realizing he was looking ahead as he pushed his horse on faster, she opened her mouth to acknowledge the plan. "As many as we can, but we also don't want to start a war if they come in peace." Isaic scoffed at the notion that there was even the possibility that peace was their purpose. From the fears of the council, Vixxen could not disagree with his pessimistic view.

6

THE FURY ISLES

The sun was higher than Juhni had expected it to be as she awoke. After swimming for what felt like forever, Juhni had finally found land, but it had been late and dark and she had not wanted to alert the Seachurns to her arrival at such a time or in an inapt means, so she had lain down on a small beach that appeared far from the main city or any of its inhabitants.

What Juhni had failed to consider when choosing her location to sleep was how easy it would be to sneak up on her. Above and beyond stood a very tall tower made entirely of crystal, and surrounding it were similar tall buildings that took Juhni's breath away. The sunlight reflected off the crystals with mesmerizing beauty, but it was her more local surroundings that broke down the sense of safety the large city in the distance created. The small beach would have slept only one other person on its orange sand, and the entire area was surrounded by large brush and fauna of species she had only heard of. A large blue flower was moving at the corner where the water and the sand consistently collided. This flower caught her gaze for a moment, and apparently, she caught *its* gaze. If the large flower had had eyes, Juhni was certain it would be staring at her.She was more certain of its living nature when the petals swayed in response to her blinking and then turned to face the water, as if enjoying the incoming waves.

Juhni felt uncomfortable then, uneasy at the idea that she was being watched by much more than a strange large flower. There was too much brush to appropriately search for any would-be attackers, so she turned and faced the sand. Although it was a deep orange color, it appeared to be similar to the yellow sand of Frendilar, which meant she could appropriately use it. She used her finger to draw a circle in the sand, taking her time to be certain it was as close to a perfect circle as possible. She then poked a hole in the center of the circle.

She looked around nervously again, looking for eyes, but the only thing that appeared to be watching her at all was the flower. It was now facing her again, its stem curved sideways as if it were watching her with an utmost curiosity. This unnerved her even though she understood that the trees and plants watched them. Her husband was friends with the Woodnips, and their magic allowed them to communicate with the trees; the trees always kept a watch on the goings-on of the forests. But this gave a whole new meaning to the idea of a plant watching her.

She returned to her drawing in the sand then, convinced that if something other than the flower was watching her, it was not about to jump her at the moment. She squeezed her thumb and finger together, and with the help of her magical abilities, she produced a drop of water from her skin and let it fall into the hole in the center of the circle. Almost immediately, the drop left the center and moved to the outer part of the circle, down, and slightly to her right.

Juhni immediately turned in that direction and stared into the brush. The speed at which the water droplet moved indicated that whoever was in that direction was close. Juhni began to find herself hoping to suddenly see a bird or other wildlife emerge from that direction, and just as she thought it must be something small, she saw them—two eyes staring back at her. Juhni's nerves erupted in fear as she reached for her rod, but she didn't remove it from her pocket.Instead, she just stared at those perfectly sun-yellow eyes.

The eyes began to move closer to the clearing, but they never blinked, and Juhni found herself taking a step back. She didn't know who or what was staring at her, and if it was a Seachurn, she didn't know what to expect; it wasn't like she'd ever met one. Her grip tightened around her rod, and she could feel her magic flowing into it as she prepared to form a weapon at a moment's notice.

The eyes vanished for a brief second as the brush moved to allow their owner to step out onto the beach. Juhni's grip relaxed almost immediately as a pretty little girl, who could not be any older than four years, entered onto the small sandy beach. The little girl was looking at her like the flower had been, full of confusion and wonder, and Juhni knew she was looking at the girl in the same manner. She was absolutely beautiful with a bright sunset-orange shine to her long braided hair and a near-perfect complexion. Juhni couldn't believe even a Seachurn could meet such beauty, and beauty and perfection were the Seachurns' way of life.

Juhni braved the first word of communication by simply offering the girl a polite hello.

The girl smiled in response and bowed in a perfect curtsy. "Good morning," she said with a bright white smile, holding on to the sides of her baby-blue dress. It was straight off with the questions afterward though. The girl spoke quickly, asking Juhni her name, who she was, and where she had come from.

Juhni had trouble not laughing in response to the little girl's curiosity. "My name is Juhni," she said, "and perhaps we can share questions 'cause I'd also like to know who it is I am speaking to."

"I'm Quixlon," the little girl said with excitement and a very happy and hyper personality. "My mom calls me Quix for short, and you're welcome to as well."

Juhni smiled at the young Seachurn's enthusiasm. "It is nice to meet you, Quixlon." Juhni got a nod in response from Quixlon, but that was the only bit of response she got before more questions came.

"Are you from the outer isles? 'Cause my mom made me meet everyone in Crystal Palace and Crystal City, but I don't recognize you."

Juhni was stunned for a moment; it was a compliment of the highest regard to be mistaken for a Seachurn by a Seachurn, even one so young, for the only thing different in appearance between the races was beauty itself. It's not that humans didn't match the beauty of a Seachurn, but all Seachurns were perfect and beautiful, at least in physical appearance. It was both a part of their race and their society.

"I'm actually from a lot farther away than that," Juhni stated. She did not get a chance to finish her statement though as another body passed through the brush into the clearing, and this Seachurn did scare her. He was tall and mean-looking and wore nothing but a pair of dark-brown pants. His muscular body reminded her of Dracut's, large and huge. He was built of power despite his lacking in height, and he had a stare that told her he knew what far away meant. Juhni was grateful he didn't lunge at her with the large sword he held in his left hand, a sword that was both larger than his body and easily appeared to weigh more as well.

"This is Zhax," Quixlon said cheerily. "He's my bodyguard. Don't worry, he won't hurt you."

Juhni suddenly knew why he hadn't attacked her even though he obviously wished to. Juhni was female, and thus, it would require a direct order from the girl for him to legally have permission to bring harm to her, human or not. It was the way the Seachurns lived, and no male was daft enough to break the gender laws. The Seachurns were known to have found the ultimate meaning for what was worse than death.

"He appears to want to," Juhni said almost smugly, partially attempting to instigate an angry response from the man.

Quixlon looked in Zhax's general direction and scolded him for his mean look. This forced a fake smile onto the muscular man, which only appeared to make him appear scarier.

"I'll cut directly to the chase with you," Juhni said suddenly. "I'm not a Seachurn. I'm a human. I've come to speak with the Ocean Queen."

Quixlon studied Juhni for a minute, her smile fading lightly, but not entirely. "You're too pretty to be a human, and my mom says humans can't travel to us without magic."

"I'm a mage, a Taille to be exact, and I've come to seek an audience with your Queen." Quixlon smiled in response then turned to Zhax and spoke to him in a watery gurgle-like language she could not even begin to understand. Whatever Quix said though certainly did not lighten his mood at all as he turned to look directly at Juhni.

"Princess Quixlon has ordered me to see to it personally you have an audience with her mother, the queen," he said with a defeated sigh. "However, the queen will not return from her hunt till dark."

Juhni was surprised to find out the girl she had met was the daughter of the Seachurn Queen, and was quite disappointed to learn that although she would receive an audience, it would take so long to do so. The face Quixlon made showed she was disappointed too.

"I forgot about the hunt," Quix said sadly. She pouted slightly. "Would you like to join me then? I'm going to meet up with my sister.She's training." Juhni felt it would be rude to turn down any invite from a princess, so she nodded and showed her gratitude to the little girl. Zhax just smiled, and Juhni wondered what the sister would be like.

⸺⬦✦⬦⸺

Juhni gripped her runic rod with strength and determination. Her hand was sweating, and she could not risk the sweat allowing her to lose her grip on her weapon. She could feel the drops of blood dripping to her lip from her nose, but it didn't hurt much, and she knew her nose was definitely not broken.

The tall blonde Seachurn came at her again; she was fast, but Juhni was used to training with her husband, who was much faster. She moved her hand quickly.The quarterstaff of water swung, and although it hit nothing but air on its first path, it found the feet of the Seachurn woman again, knocking her on her back. She slammed the quarterstaff into the ground, and the water that created it fell away, watering the soil below her feet.

The blonde Seachurn stood up and picked up her weapon of choice, a pair of metal knuckles made of a water-based gold. She shook her head with disappointment. Quixlon was sitting off to the side, clapping on her new friend.

"You are quite quick," Juhni said to Quixlon's sister, Asrien.

"Obviously not quick enough," Asrien said in response. "I can't even get close enough to hit you, and my baby sister can." Asrien was the spitting image of an older Quixlon, if the colors matched. Asrien, unlike her little sister, was blonde like the sun and had the orange fire color of Quixlon's hair in her eyes instead. She was obviously a looker though, even for a Seachurn—near perfect. Juhni had already noticed quite a few eyes watching her closely, none more than those of Quixlon's bodyguard, Zhax. It was clear that Asrien was interested in only one thing though—combat.

"That isn't entirely a fair assumption," Juhni said, patting Asrien on the back. "Your sister is twenty years younger than you, and I did not prepare for her to be that quick. I expected it from you."

"We're all quick," Asrien said immediately. "It's our race. We are extremely quick and agile. Should try this in the water where we really shine." Juhni smiled for the water was where she shined as well.

Juhni looked around the training area outside the Crystal Palace. She was still in awe of the large palace made entirely from clear crystals that reflected the sun and the water with a beauty and perfection that matched that of the two sisters with whom she was spending her afternoon. It was hard to keep her mind on the fact that she was here for urgent matters. Many times that morning, the possible upcoming war vanished entirely from her mind. The entire city was designed withbeauty and perfection; houses were made to glimmer next to the shine of the palace. It was so beautiful Juhni kept forgetting the real reason why she'd traveled such a distance.

"My mom will want to help you," Asrien suddenly said, grabbing the attention of Juhni again. Juhni turned to her and watched as she carefully tried to clean the dirt off her golden knuckles. "But sending soldiers out to help humans would need more than her okay.She'll need volunteers to fight. She can't order anyone to do so. Our army and soldiers always have a choice, unlike yours."

Juhni understood completely. Although the armies of the kingdoms of Frendilar could be ordered to fight, the mage soldiers could not. "If so many of your kind are as friendly as you are, I'm not worried."

"Lots will choose to fight," Quixlon said excitedly. She was standing behind Juhni then, and Juhni found herself jumping slightly in surprise.

"You are quite quick, and silent," Juhni said to the little girl, "but you'll scare people like that." Quixlon only smiled. Juhni couldn't help but smile as well. "My son is only two years younger than you. Perhaps one day I'll get a chance to introduce you guys." Quixlon giggled at the notion—or at the incoming gold knuckles that were flying toward Juhni's head.

With a quick back step and twist of her wrist, she watched as one fist went past her head as her water quarterstaff burst alive, knocking the other fist to the side. Then the water of her staff escaped in a burst of pressure, knocking Asrien to the ground.

"You're just so quick," Asriensaid, sounding quite impressed with Juhni's response time.

"If you think I'm quick," Juhni said with a large smile, "you should really meet my husband."

7

AMONG THE TREES

A branch nearly snapped as Jaxxal's weight landed upon it. But long before his weight could harm the tree in any way, he was in the air again, reaching for the next upcoming branch. Many years of training in agility and speed, with a discovered magic to increase both, gave Jaxxal the ability to travel quickly through the Eastern Forest undetected by even the trees themselves. The speed at which he traveled from tree to tree was just fast enough to leave behind no real trace. The lack of weight on any tree gave the trees no reason to believe him anything but a squirrel or a tratbat.

Jaxxal didn't always choose to visit the Woodnips in such an unconventional manner. Not only was it poor manners to sneak up on the Woodnips' city, but it could also be dangerous. If the Woodnips deemed him dangerous, they would kill him. Most of the time, he would literally just tell a tree he wished to meet with the Woodnips and wait for a Woodnip to come and get him. But the Woodnips were beyond patient and lacked the same understanding of time as the humans. Such a visit often took nearly a day to be collected and received by the Woodnips, and the travel to their home often took an equal amount of time. Jaxxal couldn't be sure how much time he had and was not about to risk wasting any.

Another tree buckled below his feet, giving away the possible weight of the man, but he was quite light on his feet, quite nimble, and before the actual weight could be perceived by the tree, he was in the air again, reaching high for an outstretched branch above him. His aim was solid, his grip strong—and his surprise genuine as a small black mammal screeched into his ear from upon the branch.

Jaxxal didn't get a chance to recover from the shock, and soon he found himself sitting upon the ground with a very sore rear end. The small black mammal peered down at him with eyes of pain, its bushy black tail rewrapping itself on the branch of the tree. The tratbat screeched again at Jaxxal and flapped its winglike ears in an angry tone before returning to a sleeping position on the side of the branch. Jaxxal felt awkward and sore, and a bit sorry for the creature. He had gripped its tail as if it was solely a part of the tree, and he had obviously brought it much pain.

Jaxxal had barely stood up and brushed himself off before the sound of a cut through wind warned him of the danger. Despite the lack of warning, it was plenty of time enough, and he tumbled to the side just in time to dodge what appeared to be a poorly crafted arrow. The weapon of a Woodnip was not crafted out of wood, but instead, they were grown like the trees themselves. So although the arrow appeared to be simply a poorly crafted twig with a point on one end, it was not to be underestimated for, unlike a carved arrow, this one was still alive; and immediately upon sticking into the ground, it began to grow vines out of all sides that reached out for Jaxxal.

Jaxxal was quick to react now, the shock of the tratbat's sudden appearance gone. Both his runic rods lit up quickly with a magical air, creating a nearly invisible blade of pure wind. The blade was just like the blade of any other magical weapon, equal in strength to steel or iron, but its length was deceiving, for the human eye was unable to make out the shape of the wind in which it was shaped.

The vines from the arrow retracted immediately back into itself, afraid of the sudden threat Jaxxal had produced, and he quickly began to search the tree lines for his attacker. The Woodnips were often unkind to strangers and intruders, and he had quite literally sneaked up on their home in such a way that even the trees would have only just warned them of his appearance near minutes away.

Jaxxal swayed from side to side now, refusing to stay still long enough to give his attacker another clear shot. His white mage's cloak swayed behind him, quickly moving along with his every move, and his long silver hair shot out from under his hood a few times with the motions. It began to feel like a useless tactic over time. His feet were getting tired, and he could not get even a glimpse of his attacker. More puzzling was the fact that after over twenty or so minutes, there had not been a second arrow fired at him. Jaxxal had to remind himself of the Woodnips' amazing patience.

He kept himself light on his toes, ready to move at a moment's notice—specifically at the sound of another incoming arrow, but one didn't come. The only sound that came to Jaxxal's ears was pure silence. There was no oncoming attack. Jaxxal noticed something even stranger then; the first arrow was sitting oddly still for a Woodnip's vine arrow. They rarely showed fear when attacking their target, and when they did, courage always returned in time. Jaxxal waited, but no vines came shooting back at him, even when his guard against the arrow was completely down.

"I'm not sure I have the time for games!" Jaxxal shouted into the trees. "Attack or show yourself. I must be on my way."

"Not much fun, are you?" The voice came from behind Jaxxal, and he turned around just in time to see what appeared to be a very short man, just about four feet tall. What distinguished him from a human were his colors more than his size. His skin was of a very pale green, and his hair reminded Jaxxal of a banana peel, too yellow to be considered blond.

More noticeable even was his outfit. It was designed to reveal his build and bodily features. A pair of black fur leggings that were designed to barely cover his genital regions was all the true clothing he wore. The tattoo on his left arm of a shadow tiger was the only thing that distinguished him as an elite hunter. Normally, Jaxxal would be prepared to fight such a warrior; and normally, he'd win. But there was no point in fighting a friend.

"Having arrows shot at me is not exactly what I consider fun," Jaxxal said jokingly to his old Woodnip friend, Sertan.

"I could not necessarily tell it was you. Your hood covers your face quite well. Besides, I've never met a Taille that couldn't dodge one."

"You've only ever met me and my wife," Jaxxal said with a partially scolding tone.

"True." Sertan was smiling, his off-white teeth showing proudly, and he was obviously not ashamed of the missing tooth right in front. He had lost that tooth in a battle with a shadow tiger, the Woodnips' test of elite status. Those Woodnip warriors who could tackle and fight a shadow tiger without any weapon were, from then on, known to be elite warriors.

Sertan's smile faded quickly though, and Sertan raised his bow and pointed it at his old friend. "I'm afraid I can't be too careful though. You were attempting to sneak up on the village after all, which, I have to point out, is unlike you."

"But I am but the only one you know who could do it."

"Yes." Sertan didn't blink though, just aimed, quite clearly ready to fire another arrow at any time. "I have no doubt you are you, Jaxxal. Your motives, however, scare me greatly. Why are you attempting to sneak up on us? We don't take kindly to assassins from the human world."

"I wasn't sneaking," Jaxxal said hastily, remembering time was of the essence. "I merely didn't have the time to wait for the king to send someone to collect me. You guys don't always recognize the importance of haste, but I do."

"You wish a meeting with the king?"

"And I haven't the time to wait. Lives are at stake, many lives—"

"Prepared to kill me to arrive quicker?"

A serious look appeared across Jaxxal's young features, a face that made him appear much older than he was. "No, but only because I wouldn't have to."

⊶⊷

The Woodnips' entire village was not built, but grown across the tops of the trees. The branches bent naturally in the shape of small round buildings; long flat branches stretched around like platforms, creating paths for crossing from building to building. The leaves themselves fanned out to create roofs, and vines wrapped around different parts of the village all over, growing flowers of all colors. Smaller branches grew in a spiral-like pattern around the trunks of the tall trees, creating stairs to ascend to the next level. Most humans could pass below the entire village and never even notice its existence, thanks to how high one had to climb before even the ladder-like stairs became recognizable for what they were. It took great strength and will to climb that high or the knowledge of where to find the hidden entrance inside of a hollow tree.

Jaxxal stood upon a large, flat platform in front of two large tree stumps that had grown into what could best be described as thrones. On one stump sat a small girl; she appeared to be about the age of an eight-year-old with beautiful and elegant violet hair that extended all the way to the ground below her. She had light-pink skin similar to the much older man sitting in the throne beside her. The pink-skinned Woodnip beside her was one of the tallest of the Woodnips, nearing almost five feet in height, and he sported a dark-gray beard nearly as long as the girl's hair.

"Your daughter is growing up quite nicely," Jaxxal said, addressing the king of the Woodnips. "She's, what, fifteen now?"

The young girl smiled brightly. "Getting much better at estimating a Woodnip's age," the king said.

"She looks eight. I simply doubled it and guessed something around there. It's very difficult to figure out how you guys actually age."

"It is great, gives our children more time to develop mentally before growing into adulthood."

"And allows a king to grow into a ripe old age. You're nearly 120, if I'm not mistaken."

The king laughed. "Just about, yes. With quite a few years left. What brings a young man such as yourself back to my kingdom?"

"I would expect you know. If Henriatt is at your side, then I'm guessing your wife, the queen, is ill. This, you've explained to me, is always an omen of death and war. I assume she has seen the coming ships in a dream?"

"Come to seek our aid, I'm assuming?"

Jaxxal simplynodded. He knew what the king's initial response would be, and knew it would come in the form of a lesson or speech.

"Why did Trillo, Goddess of Fury, create the Seachurns so similar to the humans?"

Jaxxal shook his head. "She liked them, I believe."

"Correct and incorrect.She attempted to perfect them."

Jaxxal knew where this was heading. He'd actually heard this speech before.

"Haidier created the Ashens to hunt and destroy the humans." The king smiled. "And the goddess of life, Gwyndle, Mother Nature herself, created the Woodnips to outlive the humans. I will not send my people to die near the ocean."

Jaxxal sighed deeply. "The landing site is not that far from this forest. You will meet them in time, and if they are hostile like we expect them to be, you'll lose many then. Would it not be better to fight them as one?"

The king said nothing at first. His daughter tugged at his arm and whispered something in his ear that Jaxxal could not hear. It did not seem to make the king at all happy. "The future queen of the Eastern Tribe invites you, Jaxxal, to stay the night while we discuss the matter with the elders."

Jaxxal wanted to protest, but he hadn't expected a hasty decision. He'd have to ride it out. His disappointment showed upon his face clearly though.

"It's much more than you'd get from the Western Tribe."

"I wouldn't enter an enemy's kingdom peacefully as I have entered a friend's. I come to you as a Taille, a human, a mage, and a friend to ask for your help to save life itself. Do you not believe my motives, Hewpert?"

The use of his name struck an immediate nerve in the king—so usedwas he to being addressed as "your majesty," perhaps, but there was an obvious amount of surprise in his eyes at hearing his name spoken aloud.

"None of which will be forgotten," his daughter said.

Jaxxal was beginning to see the influence the future queen was starting to gain even if she was many years from taking the throne from her father. She was growing into her role quite well, even speaking when her father couldn't.

"I appreciate it," said Jaxxal. "And I do hope your people have learned the understanding of haste by now, Princess Henriatt."

"We are not slow, just patient."

"I'm afraid many lives don't have time for your patience. If you wish to outlive us, perhaps you'd be better off simply killing us yourselves." Jaxxal did not know if he had played his hand over the line, and felt that playing a guilty card on people he'd always considered friends might have indeed been a mistake.

But the young princess didn't flinch or even show signs of it unnerving her at all. As a matter of fact, she smiled in response. "Find time to eat and rest, Jaxxal. The sun will set soon. When it rises again, you will have our answer." Henriatt gave him a reassuring smile and said, "I promise that I at least understand your need for a quick decision."

A QUEEN'S DECISION

Quixlon had been completely true to her word; just after the sun vanished behind the horizon, Juhni had been led to the Crystal Palace for an audience with the queen. A Seachurn male, nearly six feet tall, had led her to a small side door that she believed to be behind the throne room. It had been explained she would enter from the back and join the queen at her side. The room she currently stood in was quite tiny, barely large enough to be considered a room—a closet maybe, but not a room. Although Juhni was but the only one in it currently, she felt quite compacted in its compressed size. She understood its purpose though, or so she hoped.

Quixlon mentioned that she'd have to wait till the night's festivities began before she'd be escorted as the queen's special guest to the queen's throne. It was, however, plain for anyone to see that Juhni was questioning most of her day. She had been warned multiple times that it would be difficult to gain the trust of the Seachurns, especially those of royal blood. And yet she was expected to believe she was but a special guest to the queen.

The outer door squeaked open before she had too much time to conjure possible locations she could really be led to, and what walked into the room shocked her entirely. A Seachurn, above and beyond the age of any Seachurn she had yet to encounter, entered and closed the squeaky crystal door behind him. Not a single male Seachurn she had met yet had the slightest sign of aging; no beards, no facial hair at all. But now a Seachurn with a gray beard that nearly reached the floor, facial hair that appeared to cover up many scars and wrinkles, and eyes that showed the small, scrawny old Seachurn had seen many, many years stood before her.

Juhni was so shocked to see such an old-looking Seachurn within the palace that it wasn't until he poked her with his carved-coral walking stick did she even notice he was handing her a clean and neatly folded white cloak. "The queen felt you should wear this when you sit with her." Juhni didn't immediately look away from the bearded Seachurn, and although she took the cloak from him, it took a few seconds to recognize the golden *M* embroidered on the right sleeve.

"Where did she get this?" Juhni was absolutely astonished to be holding her mage's cloak; the last time she had seen it, the cloak had been sinking to the bottom of the ocean.

"Found it while on the hunt. She originally believed a mage had died attempting to make the journey across. Wasn't till she returned that she'd even thought it possible you'd made it." This did not make Juhni feel any more at ease.

"Been a lot of surprises since I've arrived," Juhni muttered to herself as she put the cloak on.

"Oh, what kind?"

Juhni looked at the Seachurn as though he were absolutely mad. "Never seen an elderly Seachurn."

"You're under the assumption I am a Seachurn." It hadn't occurred to Juhni that he wasn't one. As far as she was aware, humans couldn't make it to the Fury Islands, no matter how much they might want to.

"Not that I'm not," he added after a slight pause. "Just pointing out that it's your assumptions that keep making you surprised by things."

"Well, if you are a Seachurn, how old are you?"

"Onehundred and twenty-seven, with a few years left to go."

"How?"

The old Seachurn just laughed. "Bit o' dark magic, I'd have to say. Met me a few dark mages during the Mage Wars hundred years back. Learned a few tricks."

"I wasn't aware Seachurns could learn the same magic that mages can—" Juhni was quickly cut off though.

"You're still making assumptions. I learned to use a few dark items I managed to extract from an enemy. Took me years to figure out what it was, years more to learn to work it, but obviously, I managed to do just that."

Juhni didn't say anything. Using dark magic, trained or from a dark trinket, was not exactly her idea of what made a good person. The old Seachurn leaned upon his walking stick then, and she distinctly thought she saw it actually sink into the floor of the castle as he reached forward with his hand. Juhni knew it to be rude to refuse to shake it, so she reached out and shook it, not surprised at all by how old and wrinkly his hands felt.

"They call me The Old One, or Too for short."

"Does no one call you by your true name?"

"Ah, can't, can they.No one knows it." This astonished Juhni greatly. "I've been the advisor to the queen for nearly seventy years. All three of them."

"Okay, explain why my mentor received such a mixed reaction when she arrived here almost fifty years ago, and I've basically been given the royal treatment."

"Ah, guess that was a bit my fault, actually." Too shifted a bit to his right, and Juhni was positive the coral stick sounded as if it broke as it shifted with him. "See, we hadn't seen a mage since the Mage Wars destroyed a fifth of our population over fifty years earlier. I warned them to be careful in case it was a dark mage. We weren't aware they no longer existed, and we knew almost nothing about that council or the Tailles either. Now, thanks to my suggestion, we have spies amongst your kind who have given us a great deal of information on the goings-on in Frendilar."

It all seemed to make some sense to Juhni. She still had questions like why they had never thought to send scouts to Frendilar before. But Juhni wouldn't get a chance to ask another question as before she could, a loud horn sounded on the other side of the inner door, and Too began waving her along to the door.

"You've learned about our people, I hope," Too said, quickly ushering her to the door. She only nodded, wanting to point out that she'd made it to their palace. "That's good," he said before she could get an actual word out, "means less surprises."

Too opened the door for Juhni, and the brightness of the gigantic throne room nearly blinded her as he pushed her through the door. Once her eyes adjusted to the brightness of the room, she lost yet another ability—the ability to breathe for the room took her breath away. The room was so much larger than anything she'd ever seen before. Juhni had been in many large rooms in castles and within the mages' tower, but in the queen's throne room, tens of thousands of Seachurns were seated inside. They were sitting around what appeared to be a stage directly in the center of the room, which was actually down a level, so the Seachurns had to look down upon it. She noticed also that there were many more Seachurns seated below them on the same level as the center stage.

Juhni was ushered ahead to a large throne with four small thrones like seats beside it, two on each side. She couldn't see those seated in them for she was entering from behind them, but she was certain the queen was probably seated in the larger, center throne.

Juhni would have continued walking right up to the throne if Too hadn't slapped her foot lightly with his stick to make her stop. She wasn't pleased with his methods but noticed then how quiet it was for a room with thousands of people gathered close together. Silence was obviously required at the moment, and she determined that his approach to stop her was in respect for the queen.

Juhni waited what felt like forever, and it was during this time she noticed that many of the Seachurns in attendance were looking past the thrones at her. Shivers suddenly swept through her spine, and she wrapped her cloak around herself tightly in response. Too was leaning over whispering something to, whom she still assumed to be, the queen. He then looked at her and waved her to come and motioned for her to sit in the chair to the queen's right. She did as she was told, attempting to be as oblivious as possible to the many eyes that were on her.

She looked at the queen as she sat down and recognized her almost immediately; she looked almost identical to her eldest daughter, Asrien, apart from the obvious look of exhaustion in her eyes and the dawn-like orange hair of the youngest daughter, Quixlon. She was dressed in a light-blue dress that nearly looked a part of the large crystal palace she was seated within. It occurred to her then that all three of her daughters were wearing the same dress. Asrien was seated on her left, and farther to her left sat who she assumed must be the other sister she hadn't met. This daughter was the spitting image of her mother with a much younger but more sinister appearance, and Juhni found herself disliking the middle daughter almost immediately.

Quixlon was seated to Juhni's right, and just as she had been almost the entire day, the little girl was beaming happily and excitedly at her. Juhni smiled back at her and noticed her hair had been braided quite tightly. This gave her an even younger appearance. Juhni finally returned her gaze to the queen. She was yet again surprised to see a smile directed at her. It appeared that once Juhni responded with a smile, the queen rose immediately to her feet and looked upon all the Seachurns in attendance, both at their level and those seated below.

"I would like to begin tonight's important events by introducing my current guest, Juhni. She is a Taille mage from the kingdom of Frendilar, who has come seeking our aid in what she expects to be an upcoming war. Many of you have heard the rumors by now, of the boats that are currently traveling to attack them."

Juhni was astonished at how quiet it stayed amidst the entire attendance. No whispering started breaking out at these words as she had expected it to. Everyone there seemed absolutely glued to their queen's every word. Juhni was impressed with the obvious respect they all held for their queen.

"I would like to remind everyone of what history teaches us. Over a hundred years ago, a group of humans managed to land upon our shores, seeking aid in fighting off a small group of humans who had developed the ability to use magic. We didn't just ignore them, but in fear of the humans, we killed them and did not take heed to their plight at all."

Muttering started then, but it was light and between so few people Juhni could almost pick out those few who were beginning to talk to one another. The queen continued without any sign that the pure silence had been broken.

"Nearly a year later, after the dark mages had grown in number, they attacked us in an attempt to force us to fight on their side. We lost nearly a fifth of our brothers and sisters then. So I encourage all soldiers and fighters to think strongly before deciding whether they wish, or do not wish, to join in the fight. In case it helps make up your mind, I would like to announce that my daughter Asrien will be leading our volunteers into battle beside Juhni."

There was cheering and clapping suddenly from every corner of the room as Asrien stood up beside her mother. The queen did not continue to speak but allowed her daughter to take the floor. "I have volunteered to lead all warriors who wish to join us into battle. All those who wish to volunteer for this fight, I, Princess Asrien, would personally appreciate it. You have three days to decide for I don't know how long we truly have to wait."

Apparently, it was not common for a princess to join combat at all, let alone lead an army into battle. This was most obvious when she noticed the look of absolute disagreement on Too's face, who was now leaning against the wall to their far left. He was shaking his head, but Juhni was certain he was smiling while doing so. It was very difficult to discern if he was against the idea or pretending to be.

Both the queen and Asrien sat down then, and as the crowd continued noisily to cheer and talk, she leaned in Juhni's direction. "I apologize for the extremely formal meeting. I'm afraid you came on a bit of a bad night. We have a few, well, executions planned."

Juhni closed her eyes in disgust, and then she opened them and looked at the queen. "Perhaps afterward we could meet a little more informally."

"You do not have to watch," Quixlon said to Juhni's right. "I don't." Juhni turned to look at the young princess and found her staring at her feet. She didn't think she could blame the young princess because only one offense was punishable by execution for the Seachurns.

"It is nearly impossible to change laws that are founded within tradition, and since the law is based on religion, it would be treason for even the queen to speak out against it," Asrien said solemnly beside the queen. "And even the queen doesn't have the power to change a guilty verdict to innocent. So yet again, we must watch two lovers die simply because they are both female."

"It is a bit barbaric," the queen said in response, "but do not let too many overhear you, daughter. It's not yet your place to question the law." Asrien said nothing in response; she just looked at the stage with disgust.

Juhni followed the eldest daughter's gaze to the stage below to see two small glass tubes slowly rising up in the middle of the stage. Each tube, only large enough to fit a single humanoid inside, was filled with water, and inside floated a very alive and frightened-looking Seachurn. Unlike every other Seachurn in attendance, the two females in the tanks were wearing no clothing at all, although only their upper bodies were actually revealed because of the scaly tailfins that had replaced their legs. Their gills retracted and released bubbles slowly as they breathed in the water. They looked upon the crowd with both fear and hatred.

At first, Juhni wasn't sure what it was that was going on. Everyone seemed to be watching intently, and then suddenly, the water began to bubble, and the Seachurns inside began to stare at each other. They were obviously in pain, and Juhni watched as they began to bang upon the glass tubes. The tubes were silent though, and the banging could be watched but not heard. The Seachurns in the tubes opened their mouths in what appeared to be an attempt to scream, but no sound escaped the glass tubes they were in.

Juhni watched the Seachurns continue to bang, scream, and cry in pain. She couldn't even force herself to look away. She had no idea how long it went on, but it felt like forever for the two Seachurns to die in the boiling water. Time seemed to stand completely still for her until both Seachurns floated there, no longer opening and closing their gills, no longer banging on the glass or attempting to scream in pain.

The Taille mage chanced a look around at the crowd and noticed that the majority of the faces showed signs of indifference, a few appeared to be clapping, and a couple looked to be sick. She let her gaze fall upon those she sat beside.

Quixlon was still staring at her feet, obviously unsure if it was over since the entire ordeal was done in total silence. The queen didn't seem to have a single emotion painted across her face, although it didn't appear to be a look of indifference. Asrien seemed to be giving it her best ability to act just as her mother did, without any emotion, but Juhni could see the disgust on her face plain as day.

Juhni let her gaze relax on Asrien for a bit before continuing to look upon the final daughter and was sad to see that the second princess appeared to not only be okay with the execution, it rather appeared that she'd enjoyed the show. This was the Seachurn who would take the throne if Asrien never returned from combat.

Juhni felt disgusted, and she quickly looked away from the middle daughter back to the queen, who was looking at her by this point.

"Too has found a room in the palace for you to sleep during your time here. In three days, you and Asrien will lead those who wish to fight into battle. I ask only one thing, that you keep my daughter alive." Juhni only nodded, unable to so easily ignore what she had just seen. She had only once seen a human executed, and that had been done to a man who had not only murdered nearly twenty men and women in an attempt to get to the prince of the western kingdom, but also mutilated the body of two children who had attempted to stop him. She hadn't felt bad for him, but the two girls whose only crime was loving each other . . .She wished she could have done something without angering the entire Seachurn race.

9

ANCHORED IN PREPARATION

Night had fallen quickly, and where recently the sight of land had been the only thing left to view, there was a vast darkness that seemed to stretch on forever. Many members of the Xile had lost hope again as night fell, for the fear of never reaching land was just as strong as never finding it. Deerskyn had been left to choose the appropriate course in the darkness, and he didn't like his options. His shaman, Magicot, had felt a powerful change in the weather and was worried that the sea itself may be the first battle the Xile would have to fight. The best course of action was to signal to the other ships to drop anchor before the winds and the ocean itself attempted to direct them off course, or backward, forcing an even greater increase in their traveling distance.

The downside, of course, of this action had been to instill a fear in many members of the tribe who did not understand the need to wait out the night. Many saw it as a sign of uncertainty in their leader, others saw it as an omen of destruction, and most viewed it simply as a delay. Deerskyn was a proven warrior of immense courage and barbaric certainty, and as soon as the winds picked up, he knew that the dropped anchors would prove to be saviors, but his people were getting restless. It seemed as though their restlessness had increased even more so since land had been viewed, and Deerskyn knew well that his people would not be happy with any sort of delay.

Deerskyn had, of course, signaled to drop anchor. Despite the need to speed the journey, he could not take the chances of losing his direction now. It was quite apparent that he'd been right in his choice. Not but a single light could be seen in the sky;no stars could shine through the clouds that had enveloped the sky closed, and land was utterly impossible to discern through the fog. Deerskyn didn't understand enough about the sea to determine if this was because there were no lights on the land to view or if it was because the distance was too great for him to see them. If they had kept sailing at this point, they would have had no way to see where they were going,and hundreds of boats just like his were sailing behind and around him. How many ships would have been lost to them in the night had he not made the choice he had.

The sound of the waves crashing against the boat grew louder each minute, and Deerskyn paid heavy attention to them. He believed strongly in the powers of his shaman and his shaman's knowledge, and to his shaman went his thoughts now. Not a soul among the Xile Tribe had ever shown the slightest sign of powers beyond that of physical prowess except one,a man who lived a fruitful life just to die and be reborn again. It was well known that the knowledge of their shaman was years beyond any of them for he was actually capable of recalling memories from his past lives.

A footstep brought Deerskyn out of his focus on the waves.The owner of those feet were very close, and only one member of the Xile could have walked with such silence to get so close to him without alerting him. This comforted Deerskyn as he waited for his shaman to address him.

"Ready for battle, my lord?" If Magicot, the Xile shaman, had expected a simple reply to this question, then he would have been in for a shock when Deerskyn turned his head to him in obvious anger. But Magicot had coaxed the response from his leader. He knew the question itself to be of truth and yet to also be offensive to one who considered himself always ready for battle.

"And what absurdity is this question?" Deerskyn asked.

"I did not mean to insult you," Magicot lied. "I simply wanted to reiterate that information we have discussed in the past. There is a lot to remember in preparation for the coming battle. You forget I alone know what to expect on the land we sail to. I alone have visited it long ago in a past life."

Deerskyn relaxed visibly as his shaman's point became apparent. The powerful Xile leader did not tire of this conversation with his advisor. He quite reveled in what it was he had to be prepared for, knowing that most of it could save his life in the future. What use would it be to lead all his people into a battle if he did not come out of it alive to lead?

Magicot noticed the reduced hostility in his cunning leader and continued to press on when no objection was presented to him. "The humans will be your main enemy at all points in the battle. They do not compare to any one of your men or women in stature or strength, and in any one-on-one fight, your fighters will surely come out on top."

"It's in their discipline that they outdo us," Deerskyn said, an obvious venom in his voice as he said it. This was his least favorite part of his understanding of the humans. For prior to their planning, Deerskyn had always used the word *discipline* to describe his or someone's discipline to the craft of fighting, and he felt these humans could, of course, not compare. But Magicot used the word differently, explaining that his tribe members would fight alongside oneanother, but they would not be fighting together. Teamwork was the human's greatest strength; the ability to complement each other in battle could prove to be the downfall of his people,or so Magicot liked to continually point out. "We will overrun them in sheer strength and numbers," Deerskyn would always respond.

Magicot never pressed the point but changed direction immediately every time. "Perhaps," he'd say, "unless it is not just your average human you come up against. The human mages will prove to be your largest challenge. I do not know how years of peace may have changed the way the mages train and fight, but I remember mages who could single-handedly kill every man aboard this ship without receiving so much as a scratch for their effort. If we sail into a land of many battle-ready mages, we will overrun no one."

All of it was true, but Magicot knew the continent of Frendilar not to be a simple island and did not expect too many mages to be prepared for battle. He also was counting on a reduced training in combat skills because fighting was not needed in a peace-ridden kingdom.

"Do you continue to believe we should fear others besides the human mages?" Deerskyn continued to speak with anger and what was obvious to be a hurt pride in his voice.

"Not fear," Magicot smartly corrected, "but wariness of what others are capable of on the island is important. The Seachurns will surely not prove to be a challenge. They stick to themselves most of the time and do not live in any close proximity to where we will land to fight. But if they do come to aid the humans, then the battle on the sea will prove fatal to many still on the boats. The watery depths are their domain, and they will use it to punish you for every mistake made out here on the sea."

Deerskyn nodded his understanding, having been given a much more in-depth explanation of the Seachurns' powers in the sea. He continued to be perplexed by his shaman's description of their fighting prowess. "How is it they will win in a combat on land again?"

"Speed and agility will be difficult for many members of the Xile," Magicot said matter-of-factly. It was obvious to anyone that he knew exactly what he spoke of, but Deerskyn observed him with a bit of distaste for what he believed to be a disrespect for his battle prowess and the strength of his people. "No matter how hard you swing your sword at a Seachurn, if you do not make contact with your target, then no damage will you do."

Deerskyn knew he could not argue the point and turned to look out across the ocean then. He didn't listen to what his shaman said next. The conversation wore on him that night for they were so close to engaging in what he believed to be an easy battle over lesser beings. The Woodnips were the least of his worries;although their ability to use what Magicot called arrows and bows sounded scary to some of the younger members of the Xile tribe, Deerskyn felt he'd rather have one of these small sharp sticks hit him than a well-thrown ax from any member of his tribe. Deerskyn had lost even more respect for the forest-loving race when he learned of their stature, for height was a sign of strength, and these Woodnip creatures were shorter than a human, which had been relayed to him as shorter than even himself.

"I'm ready for battle," Deerskyn said with a bit of finality in his voice. Magicot had still been talking when Deerskyn spoke, but the words didn't anger him.Indeed, a smile formed on the shaman's young face. Barely having seen sixteen years, Magicot was the wisest of all the members of the Xile Tribe for his memory was old, but his body was young. He didn't argue the point of his lord; if he truly felt prepared, then it truly didn't matter to Magicot if the tribe won or lost. The shaman's only course was to bring chaos back to the kingdom of Frendilar. A hundred years without chaos, with peace, was sinful in the shaman's eyes. He'd right the sins of the humans, especially those of the surviving light mages. The Xile Tribe would no doubt bring chaos to the kingdom of Frendilar,and Magicot couldn't wait for the show. There wasn't a sight in the world better than watching chaos erupt into a million living beings.

Deerskyn could not see the hunger in his shaman's eyes, and of course, if he could, he would have taken it as a hunger for the coming battle. Magicot was a Xile after all, nearly as tall as Deerskyn and quite strong. He waved around a large and long spear in battle better than any other Xile among them, and with a hundred years of battle practice, he fought with a cunning near comparable to Deerskyn. But what truly gave the young shaman an edge was magic, a power over elements themselves. Deerskyn was counting on his shaman to get his ships safely onto the shores of Frendilar. As long as the Xile put boot to sand, Frendilar would be theirs.

10

Meeting with the Elders

Jaxxal leaned back on the wooden tree and found himself rather comfortable as the living chair of tree branches shaped itself to the curvature of his back. If it wasn't for that chair, Jaxxal would have been in a worse mood for as he sat there listening to the Woodnip elders bicker among each other, his patience continued to wear thin.

He had stopped listening to the argument the old Woodnips were having and was focused more on the inside of the largest tree house he had ever been in. Despite his friendship with the king of the eastern Woodnips, this wasactually his first time ever being inside the elders' council building, and it was quite amazing to behold. It was huge, and the leaves from the trees that bent to create the building's ceiling spread into the top of the building, giving the ceiling a nice green contrast to the wooden walls. What had been distracting Jaxxal though were the hundreds of fireflies now flying around inside just below the ceiling, giving natural light to the inside of the meeting room. This was, of course, the only light at all; a quick look outside the window reminded Jaxxal they had been sitting here for what felt like hours, and still the sun had not risen.

Jaxxal wanted a quick answer more than anyone, and he expected he had Henriatt to thank for the extremely early gathering of the elders, but he felt their lack of sleep was contributing to their indecisiveness—or, of course, it could be that it was just their way to take years to make a simple decision. It was amazing how similar a council gathering of the mages was to this gathering of the Woodnip elders; a large circular room where men and women in power argued and bickered about the appropriate course of action, almost seeming to have no way of coming to an agreement.

The council meeting that had decided to split the Tailles up to get help and information for the incoming boats had taken nearly a day to make a decision, and Jaxxal felt as if he'd be waiting nearly just as long for a decision here as well. The mage council leaders were made up mostly of younger mages, many younger than Jaxxal, and at the moment, he looked to the Woodnip princess, wondering when she would offer a younger person's view. The over-two-hundred-year-old Woodnips were a little too focused on the past wars, and Jaxxal knew that what happened in the past could not be used to determine the present.

"Could I make a quick point?" Jaxxal said suddenly, turning his head back and forth between a rather tall and thin blue-skinned Woodnip that had been enjoying a sudden shouting match with an extremely old and frail Woodnip on the other side of the room. The elders all turned to look at him. Jaxxal caught a light chuckle escape the lips of Henriatt, and he knew he hadn't been welcome to speak at all.

"We've listened to you explain the situation already. Now we are trying to determine what is best for us to do in light of it. Anything else you have to say is irrelevant." Jaxxal did not enjoy being addressed in such a demeaning way, and he was certainly not going to take it. He stood up, which was always a sore spot for the small-statured Woodnips because this forced Jaxxal to be looking down upon them.

"You continually bring up the past wars you've seen tear your people apart," Jaxxal said, ignoring the obvious stares of anger the elders were giving him, "and yet, has it not occurred to any of you that both we mages and humans do not live long enough to remember any wars. We have no experience. Do you put so much value on your lives over ours?"

"Oh, because humans have always shown that they value our lives at such a high priority." Jaxxal smiled as he sat back down, and the very outspoken woman was looking around at the other elders, a bit taken aback by their sudden silence. She turned and gave Jaxxal a death stare, but the damage had been done. Jaxxal had very narrowly avoided comparing the humans and Woodnips, but he had managed to coax the comparison out of a Woodnip elder, and this would not be overlooked easily by the other Woodnips.

An older Woodnip stood up then and walked over to Jaxxal, which made him a little uncomfortable because now that he was sitting, he was about eye level with the old, heavily white-bearded Woodnip. "For someone looking for help, you aren't going about it all too well."

"I've been friends with Woodnips for many years," Jaxxal said, "and I've never seen such a poor example of what your kind calls a value on all life than I've witnessed here in this very room from the eldest of your people."

"This coming from a man who has chosen power over his own life?"

Jaxxal didn't respond at all to this because it was a bit too close to the truth for his liking, but then again, it was a sacrifice he had made so he could help others. Jaxxal decided to look up at the ceiling so as to purposely enrage the elder. He didn't know why he was going about treating them with such hostility for it surely wasn't helping, but he just couldn't help himself. He was so frustrated with the whole process, and he hoped his wife was having better luck with the Seachurns.

Jaxxal didn't turn his head from the ceiling when he finally spoke, "As far as I see it, you have two options. You can fight alongside us, or watch us die and then fight alone. But know this. I don't forgive easily, and for every minute I have to sit here and listen to a bunch of old people bicker is a minute I could be preventing the death of a human being."

"So you'd have us sacrifice ourselves to protect your kind?" This time, the accusation was thrown at him from an old female Woodnip who was lucky the chairs were not behind a table because she was so short there was no way she'd be able to see over it. Jaxxal felt as though he had seen many a human toddler that would possibly beat the old lady in height.

"I don't ask anyone to do anything they wish not to, nor do I ask anything from anyone that I'm not willing to do myself. All I'm asking is that you allow your warriors to choose forthemselves." Silence fell in the room for the first time in hours, and Jaxxal seemed a little surprised as it suddenly appeared the elders were thinking on his request quite deeply.

"It's out of the question," said an old man, who seemed to be fighting against an immense lack of comfort in a chair that was meant to keep you as comfortable as possible.

"Agreed.Many of our warriors are too young to understand the consequences." It was fast as every elder suddenly began shouting in agreement, and it seemed they had made a decision all of a sudden. Soon, every elder had turned to their king, ready to pronounce they had made a decision.And as Jaxxal followed their line of focus, he began to laugh. Sitting in the largest chair in the room was the king, snoring lightly, fast asleep.

"Dad," said Henriatt, loud enough to wake the king up.

"Sire, what on earth are you doing? Does the fate of your people matter so little to you?" The king stood up and gave the elder woman, who had been most outspoken throughout the entire debate, a death stare.

"How dare you speak to me in such a manner!" The entire room turned dead silent, but the king appeared to be enjoying the control he held over the elders. "If anyone's value on life in this room is in question, it's all of yours. I knew how this would turn out long before I sat in this chair, and I was not interested in listening to it, but I have to at least try to follow our traditions in times such as these."

"So you left us to council and make a decision you have no intention to even hear?" asked an elder woman that had been mostly quiet throughout the entire ordeal.

"Of course not," said the king. "It was pointed out to me very early on that I needed to get better at understanding the changes in the world around us. You talk about the humans as if they are still the same people that charged into our woods two hundred years ago and slaughtered us in cold blood for wood. These are not the same humans you are all so quick to condemn, and I've decided we need a fresh perspective." He turned to Henriatt, his young daughter, who, although Jaxxal knew was in her teens, looked no older than eight years old.

She stood up and walked to the center of the room and then turned to Jaxxal with a smile on her face. "I could never force our warriors to risk their lives to save the lives of humans," she said. "But I do not have any problem with asking them if they would like to. In fact, I already have." Her father began to laugh behind her, and Jaxxal looked around the room and was rather pleased with all the faces of pure shock in the room.

"The decision amongst our warriors is near unanimous. However, they had one request of you, Jaxxal."

"Anything," he said, perhaps a little too quickly. "Well, that is to say, what do they want in return?"

"They have asked that you lead them and fight beside them."

Jaxxal felt a true smile grow on his face. "Tell them I'd be honored."

"I already did."

Suddenly, many of the elders stood up, and Jaxxal expected them to start shouting their disagreements again.

"Do not speak against my daughter's decision!" shouted the king. "It enrages me that my own people would have me turn away one of my oldest friends and allies in his time of need. My daughter, who is still just a teenager, has more sense than an entire room of our oldest members."

A Woodnip who seemed to be barely older than the king was the only elder to stay standing as the others quickly took their seats. The king stared at him, boring into him, yet he spoke anyway, "I'd like to make a request, my king."

Jaxxal realized then that he had not heard this Woodnip talk the entire morning, and as he looked closely at the man, he realized how young this elder probably was, most likely the youngest of the elders in attendance. He only looked old because he was covered in scars.

"I'd suggest you be careful what you request of me, Eggar," said the king.

"Not of you, my lord," said Eggar, "of him." And he turned quickly to look at Jaxxal. Jaxxal was taken aback. He had felt as though his role in this meeting had played its part out already.

"I am the only elder in this entire room who has ever been proud enough to fight in battle," he said, and Jaxxal recognized that his many scars were most likely there because the Woodnip had been a warrior. Most warriors, even among the Woodnips, did not survive long enough to be among the oldest of their kind.

"And what does a warrior who has survived for so long wish of me?"

"A chance to battle again." Eggar smiled a large smile as he said it, and Jaxxal could not help but notice that the smile was oddly creepy as the scars moved along with his lips. "The warriors speak of a mage who's as fast as sound. I request to join you in battle. I'm old, yes, but if I could give my life to save the life of someone who has many years left to live, it would make me a very happy Woodnip."

"I would be honored and grateful to have your experience." Jaxxal bowed slightly to the old Woodnip, who bowed back.

"Then it's settled," said the young Henriatt suddenly. "Elders, inform the warriors that if they wish to join Jaxxal in the fight for the kingdom, they should start preparing immediately." Only silence met the young girl's command, but it was a silence of obedience.

11

A RUINED LAND

Diagonally opposite the ocean-side town of Duerken, farther from it than anything else, was the ruined land that had once belonged to the Ashens. Blocked from the rest of Frendilar by a large mountain and the dark western forest, the land of the Ashens was a dead land. Nothing lived there anymore, not even a plant; and the side of the mountain that had once held the caves used by the dark mages had been turned into a straight, vertical rise—more like a cliff face than a climbable mountain.

The sun was just beginning to peek over the horizon in the morning, but in a land of mystery and death, Dracut was wasting no time in continuing forward. His camp was packed up, he'd eaten, and he was already over fifty feet off the ground. The mountainside of the dark ruins had been the dark mages' biggest defense. At the time of the Mage Wars, there had been a path, however small, but time had erased the path, and Dracut didn't have time to remake it, so he would have to scale the straight, vertical side of the mountain.

The Ruined Mountain had been carved with magic; a straight, flat, and vertical front of the mountain had been devised as a defensive mechanism. It made it very difficult to reach the cave door that had been carved as the entrance to an intricate inner sanctuary within the mountain. Dracut had barely begun his climb up the cliff face when he began to get the feeling that he was being watched. Such a feeling was often a sign of danger, but here in the ruins, it was merely a part of the location. Behind him for miles was nothing but ash—a plain of ash. No tree, no bush, no living thing had found a way to grow in the deserted land that was once home to the Ashens.

The Ashens had been a terrible race of ashy and fiery humanoids whose sole purpose was to hunt, kill, and eat every living thing. And for whatever reason, they had a powerful appetite for the flesh of humans. Dracut didn't fear them though for the Ashens had gone extinct just as the dark mages had at the end of the Mage Wars. Most people believed that the light mages were so powerful they wiped out an entire race as well as beat the dark mages to win the war. The light mages would never correct the beliefs, but no battle was ever waged against the Ashens. All evidence in existence pointed to their extinction coming at the hands of their own pet dragons. The theory was that they were kept more like slaves than pets and rebelled against the Ashens before any battle ever took place. It was hard to believe the light mages would have won the war against the Ashens and the dark mages combined.

The extinction of the Ashens and the dark mages, the only living things to ever inhabit the land south of the mountains, did nothing to calm Dracut's overactive nerves. No one had set foot in the area in decades, yet here he was. The council's hope was that the dark mages may have known of the coming fleet, and Dracut was expected to look into any information that may have survived the last century within the mountain. As he pulled himself up the mountainside another foot, taking his time to get a good foothold before releasing his grip, he couldn't help but worry for his wife. She alone would reach the port city of Lordearan before the boats would be in range of magic. And there was no way to know if the incoming fleet had magic, or even if they were hostile. But it was hard to believe in the existence of boats that size, let alone think it possible anything nice was sailing on them.

What brought the most fear to Dracut's thoughts though as he continued to climb werewhat were known to be the final words of the dark seer at the end of the Mage Wars. Before his death, the seer had been reported as having said, "Enjoy your years of peace till we return." Could the dark mages be returning now? And could the light mages stand a chance against them if they were? One hundred years of peace had greatly reduced the mages' training in combat. During the Mage Wars, combat was the only thing a mage trained in because, at the time, it was the only thing that mattered. But peace had given them the ability to study so much more such as history, nature, religion, and so many other things that would be of little use in another war.

If these thoughts, these fears, held any true grasp on Dracut as he reached the top of the cliff face, they vanished immediately because as he reached to pull himself up, he felt something grab his arm and begin to help lift him. The grip was warm, very warm—too warm. It was as though a hundred-year-old instinct awakened inside Dracut then, and he forced his body out of the grip and over the last edge of the mountain with magic. He rolled and landed a good distance away from whatever had grabbed his arm. His runic rods were in his hands already, emitting bright red fire that had already formed into the large deadly maces he fought with. He was prepared to kill without hesitation, but the living, breathing thing facing him truly made him hesitate.

Dracut had only ever imagined what an Ashen would look like, so there was no way to be sure that this indeed was a living Ashen, but it had to be. It looked like a human being with very dark hair and very gray skin. But you could see the skin slowly burning off, pieces of skin getting caught in the wind and blowing away as ash. If the gray skin was not enough to prove that this was an Ashen, then the small lines of fire that acted like veins should have been. And even if this wasn't enough to convince Dracut what he was seeing was an Ashen, then its dress surely was. Its entire outfit was of black leather and scales taken from dragons, which was the only kind of clothing an ashen could wear for long periods of time without it burning off.

Dracut's grip tightened, his heart raced, and he was sweating much more than he had been from just climbing the mountain. He had no doubts that he was face-to-face with a living Ashen, a being that was believed to have gone extinct a century ago. And then the Ashen did something that scared him even more. It smiled. Dracut gripped his mace as he looked at those long sharp teeth, designed specifically for ripping the flesh off human bone. Dracut knew nothing of the race, didn't know what to expect from it next, but nothing he'd ever read could have possibly prepared him appropriately for what was to come.

"We've been waiting for you," it said. *It.* That's what Dracut saw the being as, an *it.* A creature that was known to be deadly and dangerous. But it spoke, he spoke—no, *she.* Dracut had ignored all this at its first appearance, but although the armor hid the defining features that this was indeed a female Ashen, now that it spoke in that soft airy voice, and he really looked into its red eyes and noticed the long black hair, it became obvious that she was not an it.

"I'm sure you're surprised to see me, and you should be," she continued, as if his staring and preparation to pounce and kill her was all but a mere hello. "I did not mean to startle you. I've been watching you climb, and I was admiring your strength."

Dracut continued to fight with himself to find his voice. *How?* How could an Ashen be here, be alive.

"It is okay. I don't eat humans. And as you are a mage, I'd expect that you know that I can't eat you." Dracut became confused almost immediately. "Sorry," she continued, "but a mage's blood is actually toxic to an Ashen. So I can assure you I don't have the ability to harm you without getting killed myself."

"How?" The words finally escaped his lips, but they didn't portray his true question. "I mean, how are you . . . alive?"

"We are not entirely extinct," the Ashen said. "Me, my brother, my husband, and my son all live here in this cave. My family alone survived the dark wars, and we have tried our hardest to survive alone down here. We keep to ourselves."

Dracut recognized a softness to her voice, but his guard was up, very much up. The mace-shaped fire in his hands sparked small balls of flames as he continued to prepare for battle, but the Ashen woman just kept smiling at him.

"Please," she said. "I have watched you climb this mountain all morning, and I greatly expect you are more than capable of killing me without breaking a sweat. You've come looking for information. My daughter is special.She can see things, impossible things. She saw you coming, and my son would like to help you."

It all sounded like a trap, but he knew so little about the Ashen race it was just as possible that she was being truthful. His thoughts traveled to his wife, preparing to battle hundreds of possible warriors or maybe something worse. If there was but a chance these living Ashens could help him, help her, then he had to take that chance.

He didn't put his runic rods away, but he did extinguish the fiery maces, a show of trust that showed no trust at all.

"I wouldn't expect you to trust me," the Ashen female said. "Our people were not necessarily friendly. But we are all that's left, and we would like to help you." She watched as a piece of her ashy skin blew away into the sky, which was slowly growing dark. "Rain is coming, best get inside. Oh, my name is Profilli, or Pro for short."

Dracut did feel a friendly vibe coming on, and he recognized her truthfulness, but it was hard to quash years of believing their kind to be simple-minded monsters and trust her completely. But what could be the harm in telling her his name?

"Dracut."

Profilli smiled then. "Well, hello, Dracut. Come, meet my son." She nodded her head toward the cave entrance, and Dracut nodded in response. It was where he had intended to go anyway.

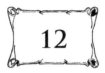

12

THE FIRST SHOT FIRED

The sky was clear now, the rain had stopped, the wind was blowing toward Frendilar, and the sun shone bright. Deerskyn couldn't be happier about his decision to anchor the night before. All of his fleet was intact and making great headway toward land, and he expected they would be in range before nightfall. His boat was no longer out in front. War was coming, and his people were getting excited, sailing as quickly as they could toward land. Men and women were armed, dressed in their leather armor and completely prepared to do battle.

Deerskyn held his large swords above his head. Both shining golden handles reflected the sun about the deck of his ship. The blades that ran nearly four feet long clanged together again and again as he rang out the sound of war for his people to hear. Weapons of all kinds clanged in response. They were ready for battle. Ten of his best ax throwers stood at the bow of the ship, ready to begin throwing those deadly axes at the shore as soon as they were in range. Things couldn't be going better.

As if in response to his own eagerness, the ocean water began to react, and the boats in front of his lost speed; one almost collapsed as the sea roared to life out of nowhere, creating a wall of water in front of them. Deerskyn recognized it for what it was. Magic. Almost as quickly as it appeared, it began to evaporate as Magicot countered the magic that attempted to turn the sea against them. As the entire wall of water became fog and gas, it let out a sound—a voice, a female voice. "Turn back around, or we will consider you hostile."

Deerskyn smiled. "We are hostile."

⸻⸻◆◆◆◆◆⸻⸻

Vixxen watched as Isaic's wall of water did nearly nothing to stop the boats that were roaring to life and gaining more speed every minute. Although they had begun an evacuation of all those in Duerken that were unable to fight, she was greatly beginning to wonder if they'd be able to evacuate entirely. The entire Duerken army was lining the shores, ready to fight to the death to protect their families,prepared to give them the time they needed to leave the city with whatever they could carry. Every horse and wagon was being used to get out food and survival equipment. It would be days till the members of the town would reach the next closest town, and it could be a whole day till they would receive reinforcements.

"Again," Vixxen said. Isaic focused all his energy into his wooden staff, asking for the sea's help to stall the boats; but though the wall stretched twice as high as the tallest boat, they crashed through it as if it wasn't even water anymore.

"It's being countered," Isaic finally determined. Vixxen understood what that meant; they had magic.

"And they aren't stopping. I get the feeling they are here to conquer." Lord Lortael advanced behind the two mages, and all three backed up a step as a wave crashed a few feet in front of them. They stood at the front lines, prepared to battle. Lord Lortael was donning his full knight's armor; all his men were donning their entire armor sets. Some of them had never battled in a full set of armor; sparring and competitions were all these men had ever seen for battle. This was going to get ugly.

"Fire!" Lord Lortael shouted. The archers on the backline fired a stream of arrows into the air, but they landed a good distance in front of the ships; they were not yet in range. In response, a few weapons, possibly large axes, came flying off the deck of the ships, but they too fell a ways short of their mark. "Looks like it's still a bit too early."

Vixxen looked at Isaic, who only smiled in response. Vixxen smiled too.Gripping her runic rod in her left hand, she focused on it; and just as it always did, flames erupted from it in both directions and formed a large longbow of fire. A black strand connected the ends of the fiery bow, and the flames of the bow moved and danced as Vixxen grabbed the black strand of smoke. Vixxen pulled it back, and as she did, flames erupted from her hands, creating an arrow of pure fire. This magical fire did not emanate heat or burn the hands of its maker.

Vixxen aimed then and said, "They are in range for me."

Deerskyn recognized what Magicot had described as arrows land in the water a ways out in the ocean. "Test the range!" he shouted. Men on the bow swung and threw their giant axes as far as they could, and although they stretched a great distance, it was clear to see that the arrows had a larger range.But either way, neither was yet in range. He had time to think, to prepare a strategy, or so he thought.

Before Deerskyn could actually start to plan how to deal with the incoming rain of arrows, another shot came from the land; just one arrow soared toward his fleet. He almost laughed.Almost.But if he had, it would have died in his throat because he watched as that one arrow landed in the sail of one of his forward ships. Upon impact, it exploded in shooting flames that landed on every part of the ship. In seconds, the ship was up in flames; men and women were jumping into the water and swimming toward other boats, away from the large fiery mess that the ship had become. And before he could give an order, two more shots were fired from the shore.

"Mages," Magicot muttered into his ear.

"So do something!" Deerskyn shouted at his shaman in pure frustration.

Magicot smiled. "As you wish." He lifted his hands in the air and began to mutter words Deerskyn didn't understand. Deerskyn turned and looked at the forward ships of his fleet and frowned as another one shot up in flames from another flaming arrow. The other ship that had been hit by an arrow was not in flames, but men and women were jumping off it as well, and he knew whatever magical arrow had collided with that boat was enough to scare and possibly kill his men and women warriors.

"Well!" Deerskyn shouted at Magicot, but his shaman did not respond; he just continued to mutter. Was their magic stronger? Could it really end before they ever even reached the shore? He began contemplating a retreat. If he never got a chance to even swing a sword, his strength and courage would all be for naught. He never gave the order though for Magicot was not attempting to stop the incoming magical arrows; he was finding a way to speed up their progress. A large wave lifted his boat up above the rest, and they rode the large wave many miles forward, greatly closing the gap between the shore and the rest of his fleet in a matter of minutes. Then the wave vanished, dropping his boat back onto the sea only a short distance from the shore. His men and women were immediately jumping from the ship into the water and charging the metal soldiers on the shore awaiting the beginning of the battle. Arrows flew at them. Deerskyn felt it as one of the sharp sticks grazed his shoulder, but he never flinched; he just charged forward. His focus was on the flying magical arrows still firing toward the other ships. He knew the mages were attempting to cut down on any possible reinforcements to the first arriving ship.

He put everything behind reaching them, but the metal-wearing humans closed off any possible path to the magical archers. Deerskyn's sword collided into the metal helmet of one human; the helmet kept the sword from cutting through the man's head, but the strength behind the blow was more than enough to kill him. A left swing from his other blade went seeking for another man, but it only collided with a large metal shield. The explosion of strength dented the shield almost in half, and Deerskyn could only smile at the absolute shock on the face of the man holding it. There was pain in there too. Deerskyn swung again, catching the nook in the neck between the armor and helmet, and that look of shock and pain was permanently etched on the face of the man as it was separated from the rest of his body.

Deerskyn never stopped, never slowed down, and never even looked around for he had but one focus. He had to reach the two mages still firing arrows into the air at the other ships. They were backing up farther and farther as more soldiers came charging forward, some with spears, some with swords and shields. Deerskyn's strength definitely gave him an advantage over the heavily armored humans. At first, they relied on trying to block his swings, but none could withstand the full force of them. But the humans learned quickly, and soon they were putting Deerskyn on the defensive as he realized that his own warriors had not covered as much ground as he had through the sea of soldiers, and he soon recognized the teamwork Magicot had warned him about. He had become a target.Arrows collided with his shoulders; his animal-skin armor did nothing to stall the arrows' travel into his flesh. It didn't matter though for he barely felt the pain as his two swords ended the life of three more men with just one swing of each. But he was not getting closer to the mages, and he quickly chose to back up so as to fight with his own warriors.

"Push forward!" he shouted,but it didn't make a difference; his warriors were relishing in every kill, and they did nothing to even acknowledge his order. His warriors had no understanding of working together or of saving his allies. They had only one focus: killing and winning against every opponent. They could not see the larger picture, and every arrow Deerskyncould not preventwas another ship down—more of his warriors who would never reach the land to help. How could he get them to understand the importance of getting through the line of soldiers?

———◆◈◆———

Vixxen fired another arrow, ignoring the already empty ship that had ridden a magic wave right to the shore. Both she and Isaic had recognized that they had an opportunity to greatly reduce any possible reinforcements. But the ships were still closing in quickly, and the soldiers on the beach were losing to the men and women already on the beach. Isaic fired just one more shot with his magical poisonous arrow. They were not stopping the boats as effectively as Vixxen burning them up. The poisonous gas they expelled surely managed to stop some, but the boats kept coming forward, and he recognized as well as Vixxen did that the front line needed their help.

"They are full of brute strength!" Isaic shouted to Vixxen over the sounds of yelling, screaming, and fighting. "Brutality at its finest."

Vixxen took a second to notice what he meant, and she could see it. The enemy looked quite human, but they were all larger, taller, and easily more muscular. They all fought with weapons of great size and weight, and she watched as one female warrior swung a large hammer and literally tossed three armored men feet into the air. They were brute strength, but they were also dressed in nothing but animal skin armor, and Vixxen knew that was very unlikely to protect them from sharp weapons. Then she saw the large barbaric woman take a hit from a spear; blood spilled from her side very quickly, but she didn't even flinch. Vixxen aimed her bow at the woman and fired. This time, the woman flinched as the magical arrow scorched the woman, burning her alive in mere seconds.

"Go," Vixxen said to Isaic. "Help them. I'll try to take down a few more ships, and then I'll join you." Vixxen knew she needed to buy time. It was doubtful that the evacuation had succeeded already. She aimed at another ship and fired, aimed again and fired again, this time releasing two fiery arrows into the air. She fired three more fiery arrows into the air in rapid succession; all but one landed in water. But the one that made contact with an oncoming ship was soon sitting still on the ocean, adding to the extreme amount of smoke that filled the ocean sky. She could only hope that the smoke would work like fog and stall some of the other oncoming boats.

Vixxen turned her attention back to the soldiers on the shore and aimed at a strong-looking barbaric woman, who had just cleared a forward path by impaling two men on her giant spear. One quick release, and the large woman's smile and joy of battle disappeared in an explosion of flames. Vixxen looked around again, searching for another open target.

13

POWERS OF CHAOS AND RAGE

Deerskyn could never have imagined the devastation that these mages could truly cause. He had, of course, understood that they were dangerous, but as he watched another one of those fiery arrows shoot across and collide into the face of a large and powerful warrior standing a few feet to his right, he flinched at the sight. In seconds, only ashes remained, and the soldier that his warrior had been fighting smiled a smile of relief. Deerskyn turned and placed his own sword right through the soldier's neck in anger and frustration at how easily his warrior had been defeated. He turned to give a seething look at the female mage who was shooting the fiery arrows, and was immediately glad he had for he almost became a smoldering pile of ash himself as he only just managed to duck below an incoming fiery arrow.

Another arrow of fire came hurling toward him again, but this time, he was more prepared for it; he grabbed a soldier by the head and lifted him up in front of the arrow. The arrow didn't have the same effect against the metallic armor. The soldier didn't turn to ash in Deerskyn's hand as he had expected. The soldier was crying out in pain as his metallic armor heated up, and Deerskyn dropped the man as he recognized his own hand start to burn from the metal helmet.

The soldier was still on the ground, screaming, and this made Deerskyn smile. He kicked the man over and then attempted to crush the man's skull with his large boots. He didn't know whether or not he had done so, although the screaming did stop, for another fiery arrow came flying toward him again, and this time he was not in reach of a soldier, so he lifted his sword in front of the incoming arrow. He felt the collision explode on the sword, and he had to grip it tightly so as not to drop it, but the heat that now emanated from his sword did not carry to the leather-wrapped handle.

He looked up at the female mage again, but she had stopped attempting to fire arrows at him and seemed to have chosen a new target behind him instead.

<hr />

Vixxen had attempted to focus her fiery arrows on the largest and what appeared to be the most deadly barbaric warrior, but three arrows later, he had countered them in ways she was having trouble swallowing. Her second arrow had erupted and killed a Duerken soldier, and her third arrow had only managed to make the warrior more deadly as his now heated sword was having a lot less difficulty with the armor the Duerken soldiers were wearing.

Vixxen changed tactics as another magical giant wave brought another boat close to the shore. It was obvious which warrior was using magic because only one was standing back, facing the ocean, half his body still emerged in water. Vixxen fired an arrow of pure fire at the boat that he'd conjured forward, but although it erupted into flames, she didn't think it truly had done anything for immediately upon getting so close, it appeared every warrior on board had already jumped off and was running through the water toward the soldiers and the fighting.

Vixxen changed tactics yet again and fired her fiery arrows at the magical warrior in the water, but the water rose in front of him like a small wall, and the fiery arrow vanished into the water. Vixxen found herself wishing her husband were here, wishing her friends were here. She felt immediately that this battle would not be such a lost cause if all the Tailles were here. She yet again found herself questioning the wisdom of the council and their decision to seek information instead of preparing to fight. She didn't have time to fathom this though for the magical warrior was focusing again on the ships still far out at sea.

She focused on the distance between her and the magical barbarian, and as he lifted his arms to carry yet another boat forward on a wave, Vixxen jumped and found herself magically closing the distance between her and the enemy shaman in mere seconds. And when she landed, her fiery bow was now a spear of fire, and it swung out at the shaman. His own spear turned around and collided with hers, but she recognized quickly that he did not seem at all happy to see her.

<hr />

Deerskyn was relishing every kill. Blood covered his body, and he didn't even take his eyes off the battle as his large boots stumbled on a body on the ground. Although his warriors were still not working together to push through the line of soldiers, it no longer mattered as a second boat of his tribe came running up the beach and joined in cutting down their foes. They were still outnumbered, but the soldiers of Frendilar were greatly outmatched.

The two large swords swung strongly together, and although they collided with a shield and sword, the brute strength in which he swung with crushed the body of a soldier. There was a chance the soldier had survived, but it was no matter; he was no longer in a position to continue to fight, and Deerskyn stepped over the body to attack yet another victim. Immediately, he felt pain, true pain. He did not understand these humans. The Xile were a people who understood defeat as just that, but the humans were fighting for so much more, and their defeat was not final as long as they still could draw breath. With his final one, the crushed soldier had slashed through the back of Deerskyn's boot and shin.

Deerskyn had focused too long on that pain; it was truly shock more than pain that caused the pause, but three soldiers came at him then, and he took a few more cuts to his arms as he failed to right himself and parry away the incoming swords. There was no way to know if Deerskyn would have ever been able to recover from that shock.He was truly in a tight spot, but his son came through for him then. A spear twice the length of any spear used by the Frendilar soldiers passed by Deerskyn and skewered a soldier right at his neck, right under the helmet and above the armor. His son's spear didn't even bother to shake off the body before smacking another soldier over the back of the head, knocking him aside and leaving only one soldier for Deerskyn to worry about.

Deerskyn smiled then as both his large swords caught underneath the arms of the remaining soldier who was attacking him and lifted him off his feet. He turned one sword over and didn't even flinch as he removed the solider from the world permanently.

Deerskyn turned to his son, a smile on both their faces. Deerskyn almost didn't see it coming; a long vine was shooting right at him, and he just barely managed to avoid getting hit by it. Deerskyn wished almost immediately that he had not avoided the vine-like whip that stretched far past him for its intended target had not been him, but his son. His son's spear was no match for the magical vine as it quickly wrapped itself around his son's neck.

Deerskyn's burning-hot sword sliced through the vine quickly, but it didn't do anything for the part of the vine that was still wrapped around his son's neck where it continued to tighten, and blood poured from his son's neck. He left the battle then;he ignored an arrow that flew past him, spilling blood from his cheek. He knelt beside his son and began fighting to pull the vine off his son's neck, but it only seemed to squeeze tighter, and he was unable to stop it. Unable to do anything at all, he watched that thorned vine cut through the skin and then the bone, and the fear and pain were left permanently etched on his son's face.

———◆◇◆◇◆———

Vixxen dropped to her knees as the spear crossed above her head in a large arc. She quickly attempted to counter by sweeping the magical warrior off his feet, but he was quick, and her fiery spear passed harmlessly below him as she just continued with the momentum she'd created, spinning around and standing up as she went. Her next swing collided with a wall of water, and the smoke and steam that erupted from her weapon was probably the only thing that saved her from his counter as she dropped and rolled.

The shallow water slowed her roll, and once she was standing, she was soaked. She could already feel the additional weight of her wet cloak. Vixxen did her best to balance herself against the extra weight as the magical warrior came at her again, swinging his spear quickly and forcefully, and it was all she could do to act defensively against it. Again and again, she felt herself being pushed deeper into the ocean; and from that angle, she could see everything, and she wondered how strange her battle must seem as she and her opponent battled knee-deep in the ocean, battling both each other and the small waves crashing over them.

A wave hit her just as she saw a possible opening in her opponent's stance, and she was knocked forward. She couldn't help but recognize how unlucky she'd gotten. As she turned around, her back now to the beach she quickly realized that it had nothing to do with luck as two more waves crashed into her, one after another. Smoke rose all around her as the magical fire that made up her spear collided with the water. She focused her energy into her spear, and with a burst of air, cleared the area around her of the dark black smoke—just in time to see that dark silver spearhead come swinging at her head.

———◆✦◆———

Deerskyn's anger, pain, and pure brutal rage had increased his strength and his determination as he once again attempted to push through the Frendilar soldiers to the white-hooded mage who had killed his only son. With one swing of his right sword, three knights lost feel of the ground as they were tossed brutally into the air. If he'd had any control left of his actions, Deerskyn would probably have marveled at his own strength at that moment as he forced another three knights off their feet with a brutal swing from his left sword. He didn't even feel the arrow that suddenly hit him, piercing deep into his shoulder. It didn't have any effect on him at all as both his swords swung out in front of him, and a shield went flying in the air to his left, and a helmet flew to the right. The defenseless knights quickly found themselves dead from another mighty swing of his deadly swords.

Pain shot through Deerskyn's arm suddenly; unlike the arrow, he noticed this sudden pain, but perhaps it was more because the thorny whip that had hit him alerted him to how much ground he had truly gained. And now he had suddenly come upon his prey. The next pass of the mage's whip passed by him harmlessly as he sidestepped to his right, elbowing a knight in the head as he did so. He barely noticed his sword following through and drawing large amounts of blood from that knight's neck. Deerskyn's eyes never left his true target.

The thorned vine whip collided with the ground, feet in front of him, and he almost laughed for he could not possibly have predicted that it would travel through the ground and erupt below his feet, wrapping tightly around his ankle. Anger and pain forced him to cut the vine just as he had done to try and save his son, but that reaction did nothing but return the whip to its owner while the remaining piece that wrapped around his ankle continued to tighten, drawing blood and spilling it all over the ground. But just like all the other hits Deerskyn had received, it didn't faze him in the slightest as he continued to press toward the mage. And as he finally made his first swing, he smiled as he felt a rush of excitement. His excitement, however, vanished quickly for the vine-like whip changed shape in less than a second, becoming a long wooden club, and somehow, that scrawny, unarmored mage had stopped his follow-through completely.

Deerskyn came forward quickly swinging with his other sword, and yet again, that wooden club parried the swing, and all the brute force he could muster came to a stop upon colliding with the club—and in almost the same instant, it became the whip again. Deerskyn could not react fast enough to stop it from swinging up and wrapping around his neck. He immediately felt the pain from the sharp thorns, and for a brief second, he almost gave up then and there. But he had one option, and instead of trying to cut the vine with his sword or trying to grab at it, he jumped forward. The weight of his entire body crashed on top of the scrawny mage.

It was almost as easy as squashing a bug. The magical club had been able to fight off his sheer strength, but apparently, the mage's body did not have the same ability. With one quick swing of his head, he could feel the cracking skull of the puny little man who had killed his son with cheap magical tricks. Deerskyn didn't understand a lot about magic, but as the vines that had been squeezing around his neck and ankle released, he knew that he'd avenged his son's death.

14

WARRIORS OF THE SEA

Juhni had been handling herself as best she could throughout the night and next morning, but the beauty of the crystal city was slowly diminishing as she worried about her friends in Duerken. With every passing hour, she heard nothing new, and Juhni wondered if she could survive doing nothing for three days while she waited for the Seachurns to decide whether or not they wished to swim north to help fight a war.

Even the beauty of the crystal palace was slowly diminishing in her eyes as she wandered through it. Her wait during the day had become a bit of an exploration as she checked out the magnificent ballrooms and dining areas. Many Seachurns had stopped her in the halls to ask about the mainland and Frendilar, and she had been happy to oblige them with answers. The palace was full of statues made entirely of diamond and crystal, and she had been stopping and taking each and every one of them in all day long. It had been a true sight to see earlier, but as the day grew on, her patience waned, and even the beauty of the palace had begun to lose the ability to distract her. She didn't know what was going on in Duerken; all she knew was that people could be dying, and she was doing nothing.

Juhni's concentration had vanished as she continued to wander the palace until a young girl shouted her name. Juhni had just turned a corner, and she looked ahead to see the youngest princess, Quixlon, running toward her.

"My mom wishes to speak to you," Quixlon said excitedly. Juhni smiled; if there was but one thing on the entire Fury Isles that could get her mind off the war, it was this little girl. She was so beautiful and so innocent that Juhni's motherly instincts could erase her worries as she wanted to secure that innocence in the small princess.

Quixlon grabbed Juhni's hand and, with much excitement, pulled her into the queen's private chambers.

"Ah, that was rather quick," said the queen as Juhni and Quixlon entered.

"She was in the hall," Quixlon said, still with her excited little girl's voice. Juhni's smile lingered as Quixlon jumped onto her mother's bed to sit beside her.

"Do you have children, Taille Juhni?" the queen asked as she began to brush the bright-orange hair of her daughter.

"I have a son," Juhni said. "And the formalities are not necessary, your majesty."

"Please, if I am to address you only by your name, then do me the decency of doing so as well."

"Very well, Rubi," said Juhni. "He is a couple years younger than your daughter here."

"When was the last time you saw him?" Juhni gave the queen a slightly hurt look, and the queen quickly apologized. "I am sorry. You do not question our ways. It is rude of me to question yours. Children are a great gift"—Rubi paused as voices carried down the hall—"and sometimes a burden."

Juhni recognized the voices that were carrying into the room from the crystal hall. Asrien was shouting something at her other sister, and they certainly did not sound like they got along very well. The voices grew closer, and Juhni could just make out what Asrien was saying. "You don't know anything!" the oldest princess was shouting. "And Mom doesn't have time to listen to your rants."

"Don't worry. You can't keep it a secret forever."

"I don't have a secret!" shouted Asrien as she turned into her mother's chambers. "But we have more important things to discuss with Mother anyway."

As Ferdile followed her sister into the room, it was apparent she wanted to quickly tell her mother Asrien's secret, but the queen seemed not to care. "Your sister is quite right," she said, addressing Ferdile. "Please leave us alone to talk. You can help by finding my advisor."

"That's not fair, Mom!" Ferdile began to shout. "She—"

But whatever she was about to say, Juhni didn't find out as Asrien quickly put a fist to her younger sister.

"Girls, this is not the place!" the queen shouted angrily. "Ferdile, get out!"

Ferdile's disappointment and anger were clear upon her face, and she gave her elder sister a look of pure hatred before storming out of the room, holding a hand over a bloody nose.

Juhni looked to the queen, but she didn't appear angry or even curious, just concerned. "Should I be concerned?" she asked her daughter.

"Of course not, Mother," Asrien said as she closed the door behind her fleeing sister. "You know how she is."

"Of course," Rubi said, now turning her attention back to Juhni. "Now that Asrien is here, I can tell you why I wanted to speak to the two of you." Juhni recognized an urgency in the queen's voice, but the change in conversation made Juhni all the more curious about what was going on between the two older sisters.

Rubi stood up, leaving her youngest daughter to sit calmly alone on her large white bed. "I'm afraid we are going against my prior word."

"But, Mom—" Asrien was quick to assume, but the queen raised her hand; Asrien closed her mouth, but there was a sign of disappointment on the eldest princess's face.

"It's not what you think," the queen said, ignoring her daughter's outburst. "We were going to wait three days to give the warriors a chance to make a decision, but we do not have the time. Siran has informed me that the ocean is screaming in terror. This war you feared, Juhni, has begun."

Juhni's heart sank as her fears were confirmed for the first time. "I must go then."

"Yes," said Rubi, "and Asrien will join you with every warrior who wishes to. They just do not have time to decide, for the journey to swim that distance could take too long. If we wish to help, you must leave at once."

"I'll spread the word," Asrien said, quickly turning on her heels and heading for the door. "We will be in the water within the hour. And at full speed the whole way, we might be able to make it in a day's time." Asrien nodded to Juhni and left the room.

Juhni turned to follow, but the queen stopped her for a moment. "Please," said Rubi, "I may not be certain of my daughter's motives in this, but I have made a guess. Don't forget what I asked of you."

"Don't worry, I'll make sure your daughter returns safe and sound," Juhni said.

Rubi shook her head though. "Just promise to keep her safe. Returning will only be up to her." Juhni did not understand, but she nodded, turned, and left. Only moments later, she found herself regretting that she did not say good-bye to the youngest princess who had found her on the seashore the prior morning.

15

WHIPPING WILLOW

The black-and-silver spearhead was aimed directly at her head, but Vixxen had seen it soon enough to avoid taking a direct hit. Her reaction greatly reduced the sting as it just scraped against her ear. Her dodge had been unexpected by the shaman she was fighting, and as he lost his balance in the follow-through of his forward thrust, Vixxen was able to come around to the side of him. Her thrust ignored the magic barrier of water that came up to greet it, stabbing through it and, in a cloud of smoke, making contact with the leg of her opponent.

Vixxen would be the next one to lose her balance though for she had expected the collision of her spear with human flesh to erupt her foe into flames, leaving nothing but ash. But her opponent had obviously protected himself against such magic, so her spear did nothing but act like a normal spear would—break a bone and pour the warrior's blood into the ocean. Before she could get a chance to finish the job, another magical wave collided with her body. She was not able to grab a true and balanced footing and quickly found herself caught in the undertow of the wave. Her body and, more importantly, her head hit multiple jagged rocks on the shallow bottom of the ocean as the water determined her course. She was fighting with her body to right itself and doing everything she could to attempt to breathe, but there was no oxygen below the surface of the water.

It happened before she knew it; oxygen filled her lungs, and her foot found ground, forcing her to stand up in very shallow water. She could feel a lot of pain now as the salt in the water made the many open cuts she now had sting as if her wounds were ablaze like her magical spear. It was then that she realized that the wave had dropped her focus, and she was no longer holding a fiery spear, but just the hollow metal rod she'd created as a teen. She focused, quickly reigniting her weapon, the flames erupting in both directions from the rod to once again form her magical spear, but her speed and haste were unnecessary for the warrior was still deep out at sea and was swimming away from her, not swimming toward her.

Although his wound was most likely worse than her own, she was beginning to feel her strength and focus draining away with each drop of blood that she lost. Each drop that joined the sea took some of her energy with it. She turned to the battle on the shore to find that although no more boats had yet joined in the fray, the barbaric warriors were pressing up the shore toward the town, and the soldiers of Duerken were retreating. And then Vixxen noticed something that made her heart stop; the soldiers in the front line were forming a wall as the rest of the soldiers were not just retreating, but straight out running away. There was only one thing that could create that sort of fear in a human soldier, and since Vixxen was still alive, she knew who wasn't.

Deerskyn's face was solemn and serious as his rage was far from abated, but the rest of his tribe did not share the same stern, angry look. They weren't sharing his grunts of anger and his shouts of fury; they were taunting his feelings, his loss with cheers and laughter. Each of those soldiers that were running away was a murderer who was escaping fate. His tribe might be finding their cowardice comedic and dishonorable, but Deerskyn saw it differently. He saw each soldier that was running away as one who refused to accept the fate he himself had chosen for them. They were cheating death— death at his own two hands. But as he swung both of his swords at the wall of shields blocking his path, he only moved them back an inch. The magical heat of his left sword was gone, and the large metal shields were proving difficult when placed together in such a defensive move.

A large Xile Tribe woman managed to push past the edge of the wall of soldiers, knocking down three of them that had made up the very end of the wall; but upon doing so, she took four well-aimed arrows to the face from the retreating archers, and she did not get a chance to relish in her success. Deerskyn slammed his entire body against the wall, and although one soldier fell to the ground and lost the use of his leg as Deerskyn crushed it with his massive foot, the wall of soldiers collapsed onto the new weak point, and Deerskyn found himself only getting frustrated at the suicidal defensive move. The soldiers were not even attempting to mount an offensive as they blocked the Xiles from pursuing the retreating troops.

If Deerskyn could have understood that the human's sudden decision to retreat had not been caused by their obvious defeat, perhaps he would have acted against the wall with tactics instead of constant attempts of brute strength. As it stood though, by the time Deerskyn knew what had truly caused the soldiers to retreat, it was far too late to even think about chasing after the fleeing enemies. The entire ground began to shake, and not just from the many large, barbaric bodies slamming against a wall of shields. It was something unnatural, something that Deerskyn knew must be magical in nature. At first, he managed a smile, assuming that Magicot was about to magically bust through the wall, allowing him and his tribe to quench their bloodlust by cutting down the many cowards running for their lives. Deerskyn was greatly disappointed though when he turned around and found that his trusted shaman was nowhere in sight.

The female mage who had been fighting Magicot one-on-one out in the ocean itself had just vanished, and Deerskyn could not make out his shaman anywhere among the waves either. Before he would get the chance to look harder at the moving waves though, the ground shook again, and he found himself falling face forward onto the ground. He heard metal colliding loudly behind him as the ground shook yet again.He turned to look for the sound as he attempted to lift himself off the ground and found that the wall of soldiers and shields had fallen, but so had most of his warriors.Before he could get himself even partially off the ground, he found himself face-first again in the sand on the beach; and as he lifted his head in the direction of the dead bodies behind him, he knew fear for the first time in many years. Just as suddenly as the ground had begun to shake, an explosion of sand occurred from underground on the beach, and out of the sand erupted a tree trunk of a thickness that rivaled the size of Deerskyn's prized boat.

The tree grew from the sand so quickly that in less than a minute, the ground stopped shaking, and a tree taller than any building, boat, or even surrounding tree stood directly rooted where so many dead bodies had just lain. Deerskyn finally was able to find his feet, but the large weeping vines that made up the tree's branches did not allow him to keep his balance as they wrapped around his feet and quickly swung him sideways. For a second, his head dragged across the sand, and then he found himself soaring through the air out into the ocean. He came up for breath quickly, but a wave crashed over his head; and before he had a chance to look again at the mighty tree, he was fighting for breath underwater again—and just as quickly, he found himself breathing above the water yet again, bearing witness to a sight unlike anything he had ever seen before.

The giant weeping willow did not recognize the difference between friend and foe as its branches grabbed Duerken and Xile alike, some being flung into the ocean, some onto the dock or into boats, and some never being let go and simply being constantly smashed into the ground. Once the threat of the long vine-like branches became recognized by all those around, the ground began shaking again, and the roots of the tree began erupting from the ground all over the beach, crushing and stabbing every single living thing it could find. Deerskyn recognized then how lucky he had been to have landed so far away in the ocean. Even though he found himself yet again fighting below a wave he could not control, the power of the sea seemed minimal to the power of that gigantic and powerful tree.

It swung and thrashed and within minutes, that single tree had crushed and killed the majority of the forces that had followed him onto the beach and almost the entirety of the remaining soldiers that had sacrificed their lives so that so many of their neighbors could survive. Deerskyn knew that this tree had been what the soldiers had feared, but who had created it? Everything that Magicot had told him about the humans could not bring him to believe a mage would sacrifice so many men with magic they could not control. But if it had not been a mage, then how had the soldiers known to retreat before the ground had even begun to shake? Deerskyn contemplated these thoughts as a metal helmet landed in the ocean a few feet from him, a helmet that was still being worn by only the head of a Frendilar soldier, and Deerskyn could not deny that this would surely delay the rest of his tribe from putting boot to land.

Vixxen stared in absolute horror at the destruction the magical weeping willow was enacting on both the soldiers of Duerken and the invading warriors. She absolutely couldn't believe how much magic had obviously been built up inside of Isaic for the battle, and she quickly began contemplating how much devastation her death could have caused if she too were to have died in battle. Isaic, of course, had warned the soldiers of what could happen if he or Vixxen were to die during combat, but even he could not have predicted how terrible it would be.

Vixxen had witnessed in the past small explosions of light, small balls of fire erupting into the air, and, on one occasion, a small twister that blew around the contents of the mage's library, but no one had ever witnessed what happened when a Taille died in battle. Because unlike most mages, the Taille had trained for years to focus and store magic in a single place, allowing them to call upon strength and power at a moment's notice if need be. It was supposed to be used in an emergency situation, but just like all other magic stored up in a mage's body, it had to release upon the end of the body holding it in place.

"I have never seen a more horrifying display of magic in my life." Vixxen jumped almost a foot forward as the lord of Duerken came up behind her at the forest's edge then. She had been so focused on the tree that she had ignored the many soldiers still fleeing into the woods, leaving behind their home and hoping to find and meet up with their families somewhere along the road.

"We knew it was dangerous to bottle up so much magic, but it was supposed to be used to protect us in tight situations."

"I do not think a soul will blame you or Isaic for this destruction. On the contrary, it has bought us time," Lortael said. "I was commenting more on how you were looking at it than how I was."

"Isaic was not the only one of us that tempted to test the limits of how much magic we could store," Vixxen said with tears now running down her cheeks. "If he knew that the release of all that magic killed many innocent lives—"

"Luckily, then, he will never know. I suppose that is the beauty of such magic releasing after death. If you weren't worried about it before, you sure aren't worried about it after." The statement was made slightly in jest, but Vixxen could find no laughter in her, no smile, not even half a grin. She'd lost a good friend, and his death had been the cause of more loss of life. "How did you escape?" Lortael asked. Vixxen turned to look at the leader of the town then and shook her head, allowing herself to recognize then that she would not cause the same kind of destruction.

"I teleported," she said as if it had been obvious.

"I did not know mages had such powers."

Vixxen looked again at the weeping willow that now marked the corpse of a dear friend, and when she answered the lord of Duerken, it came with a seriously grim undertone, "Built-up magic can do things no human should have the power to do."

Lortael understood the implications of her statement, and beyond the relief of learning that she had survived the initial battle, he was relieved to recognize that she was no longer a walking bomb. And although her death would greatly reduce morale among all those fighting beside her, it would not immediately culminate in their deaths.

16

THE ASHENS' DEN

Dracut was as far from the battle as it was possible for him to be, deep in a mountain on the opposite corner of the continent. His focus remained on the female Ashen and the spooky, dark maze of a tunnel they were traveling through. Every time Profilli took a fork in the tunnels, Dracut found himself attempting to make a mental note of the choice but quickly found there were just too many forks to remember how to get out. He knew they were getting deeper into the mountain as they walked, but every now and then, the tunnel passed the outside edge because he could hear the sound of the rain that was falling outside, as Profilli had predicted it would.

The stone that made up the walls of the tunnels was difficult to make out in the glow of the torches that lined the walls. Dracut kept stopping to examine these torches because they were unlike anything he had ever seen. The fire that flickered from the torch was not orange, red, or even yellow as one would expect fire to be. These special Ashen torches were alight with a dull violet flame that only made the tunnels appear dark despite being well lit. As he had done many a time, Dracut stopped at one of these torches as they turned a corner and tried to determine what was making the fire turn such a color, and for the first time, Profilli stopped as well.

"Fascinating, isn't it?" Dracut turned to her and nodded his agreement. *Fascinating* was truly a good word to describe what he thought of the purple flames.

"What makes the fire burn purple?"

Profilli laughed lightly, and Dracut noticed in the violet light that her face seemed different when she laughed, almost as though it had worn from many years of life. However, the minute she finished laughing, she looked just as young as she had when he'd first met her on the cliff top.

"Sorry, I suppose it has been years since anyone has seen such fire.It's dragon fire." Perhaps it was clear on Dracut's face that this did not explain a thing for she quickly continued, "Dragon's breath fire and the fire they breathe is always purple. When you light a dragon's spit or sweat, it lights purple just like its breath does. It's not as bright, and it doesn't give off much heat.However, it is deadlier, and it lasts much longer. We haven't relit the torches in the tunnels in at least three years."

Dracut turned and looked at the torch again; he had, of course, known that dragons breathed fire, having heard many stories of the beasts as a child. However, not one of those stories had ever mentioned the fire to be different from the fire one lit for cooking or to keep warm on a cold night. Of course it made sense that it would be different now that he thought about it. The stories had often mentioned that a dragon's breath could melt a knight's armor in seconds, so why had it never occurred to Dracut before that the fire must be different from natural fire.

"Coming?"

Dracut quickly turned around, having gotten lost for a second in the motion of the violet flames. He nodded, remaining void of emotion, reminding himself that he was in a very dangerous situation. There was no reason to believe that this woman meant to harm him, but then history gave him no reason to think she had any intention of letting him leave these tunnels alive. Dracut was at war with himself, morality telling him that he had to treat the Ashen like a human and not like a monster. But a whole other part of him knew that he could wind up dead if he didn't watch her with the utmost care.

So as he'd done for the entire morning, he followed her through the tunnels, often worried that she was leading him into a trap. He half thought she was expecting him to forget his way and never be able to escape the mountain caves. His runic rods were still held steadily in his hands for his own protection, and just as he began to grow truly paranoid of the intent of the Ashen, they turned a corner into a large open room most likely near the center of the mountain. The tunnels had forced Dracut to duck many times so as not to scrape his head upon the ceiling, and now he found himself in what was unmistakably designed to be a meeting point within the tunnels and caves. The room was massive, and as Dracut looked up to the ceiling, he almost chuckled for even with a magical boost, he didn't think he could reach high enough to touch such a high ceiling.

Dracut's eyes left the ceiling and fell upon a large black stone throne on the other side of the room. The Ashen sitting in the throne had not initially been what had drawn his gaze; initially, it had been the purple flames that surrounded it, but now that he truly looked at the male Ashen seated so comfortably in the throne, he knew immediately why Profilli had appeared old when she had laughed. She *was* old. The new Ashen was only slightly taller and, to the untrained eye, looked no older or younger than Profilli, but Dracut recognized the dark-gray skin that was not flaking at all. His veins, too, shone a much brighter red and resembled lava more than blood. The skin gave away his youth, and Dracut did not need to know that to recognize it then.

"Dracut," the Ashen said, standing up and walking away from the purple flames and the black stone throne. "I've been waiting for you." Dracut said nothing, just stared at the Ashen with a look of indifference, which was a subtle way of saying, *I definitely don't trust you.* The Ashen seemed to ignore the obvious hostility in Dracut's facial expression and just continued walking toward him. The Ashen had a large smile upon his face, which did not bring comfort to

Dracut at all as those long, sharp, pointed teeth and fangs glinted in the purple glow.

"We have been waiting for you for some time," the Ashen said, stopping mere feet in front of Dracut. The Ashen was much taller than Profilli and had a mane of long black hair that blended in with his dark-gray skin as if he had been wearing a hood. But despite the color of his skin and the smell of burning flesh that emanated from the Ashen, Dracut recognized how human-like he was.

"My name is Shavore, but I'm sure my dear mother has already told you all about me." Dracut shook his head. "Truly, whatever did you talk about on the long trek through the tunnels?"

"Wasn't really up for talking," Dracut said, finally speaking to the Ashen who had just introduced himself as Shavore.

"I understand. It must have been a bit of a shock to find out that a few of us were still around, especially after so many years." This statement only created more questions in Dracut's mind, which was most likely not Shavore's intention. Not just how they were alive or why they were in hiding, but more than anything, Dracut wondered why they hadn't killed him already.

"I expect you have not heard friendly things about my people," Shavore said, sighing and shaking his head slightly. It was a simple gesture, but Dracut found himself ready to, at a minimum, listen. Perhaps he was not ready to trust the Ashens, but he needed to know what they knew.

"Your mother," Dracut said, looking over at Profilli, who was leaning against the corner of the entrance behind him, "said you could help."

"Ah, straight to business then." Shavore smiled again, but this time, the smile was small enough not to show those sharp teeth, and it appeared to Dracut as a much friendlier smile. "Very well, but let's not talk here. It's a bit much." Dracut looked around the large open room and did feel rather small. It made him feel as though he was standing in the middle of a mountain, which of course, he was. But the tunnels had felt cramped, like being underground. This room truly felt like standing in a hollowed-out mountain. "This way. There is a much smaller room over here. I suppose I could have waited for you in there, but I wanted to make an impression." Dracut noticed that the Ashen never relinquished his smile, and Dracut was slowly but surely begging to release a lot of the tension he'd built up since running into a breathing, living Ashen.

It didn't take long to enter the smaller room, and before Dracut knew it, he was sitting in a chair carved out of stone. Shavore seated himself across from him, a large table of stone between them. His mother, however, chose not to sit and seemed to be more inclined to fade into the backdrop as she stayed close to the door they had entered through.

Dracut's guard was far from dropped, and within seconds, he'd already recognized another stone doorway leading farther into the mountain. He knew if he needed to run, his best bet would be the way he'd come in because there was no reason to think that the other way led to an exit. This fact helped fuel his paranoia as he recognized the fact that the female Ashen, Profilli, had indeed chosen to stand, almost as if guarding the very door he'd need to flee through. Perhaps it was this reason that he did not return his runic rods to his belt but turned them over in his hands instead. It was a subtle motion, but he wanted this Ashen to know he still did not trust him and that he was armed, and he hoped that the dangerous weapons in his hand would let the Ashen know he was indeed dangerous.

"I don't expect you to trust me," Shavore said, quickly addressing the obvious tension in the room. He then turned to his mother and nodded his head; the motion released a small bit of skin that floated slightly away before burning up. It was still a strange sight to see. It had been much more constant with the older female Ashen, and perhaps because of that, it almost seemed strange when Shavore's ashen skin released like ash from a campfire. When Dracut finally turned to the doorway, he realized that Profilli had left. He and Shavore were alone, and the escape route he had initially devised was no longer blocked.

Shavore turned back to face Dracut, and he appeared so relaxed. Dracut couldn't help but feel a little less tense as he finally addressed the Ashen, "So you know why I'm here?"

Shavore nodded. "My sister sees things, kind of like your seers do. I suppose the difference is she has no control over her powers. You're here because of the boats." Dracut did not say anything in response, and yet again, he found himself distracted by the ashen skin peeling and floating away. He shook it off and recognized that Shavore had said something else.

"Sorry," Dracut said.

Shavore shook his head. "Don't be. I can only imagine how disconcerting my appearance must be to you. As it is obvious I am not like you, and although they may appear it, those who travel on the boats are not like you either."

"Do you mean"—Dracut paused, attempting to find the words he wanted to say—"they are not human?"

"Depends on how you define *human*." Shavore's response caught Dracut entirely off guard. How does one define *human*? "Let me see if I can explain what I mean. What do you know of the gods?"

"Well, I know a lot," Dracut said as if the question was an insult to his intelligence and knowledge.

"How many are there?" Dracut didn't even stop to think, didn't even wonder why the question was being asked; he just held up four fingers and was immediately shocked that Shavore shook his head in response. "You only know of four because you have only ever had contact with those that believe in them. The animals and plants were the first life the gods created, but after much time, Totailon, or the god of war as you know him, attempted to create life closer to that of the gods."

"I know the story," Dracut said, trying not to sound as if he was being defensive, although he knew he had failed. "Totailon created humans."

"Yes, that is true," Shavore said. "But the point I was trying to make is that if you define a human by the characteristics of what

Totailon created, then even I am human." Dracut didn't even have a thing to say. He knew where this was going immediately. The gods followed Totailon's example, and each one created their own race entirely based on the humans. Trillo made the Seachurns in an attempt to perfect what Totailon had created. Haidier, the god of hate, made the Ashens in an attempt to sow hate and fear into all living things. And of course, the goddess of life, Gwyndle, created the Woodnips in fashion with all life, not just that of the humans. However, the obvious point was that they were all created based on the same model, Totailon's first creation. Dracut would never have considered that an Ashen may indeed be human, but despite not being *a human*, it was clear that he could not overlook the similarities between the different races.

It's at this point in the silence that Dracut truly knew what was on the boats. "They are another race?" He said it like a question, but he already knew it to be true, and Shavore nodded in acknowledgement.

"There are six gods in total, three couples," Shavore said. "Juliesse, the goddess of peace, is known for staying hidden and in the background, but more often than not, she is in control."

"Peace, so these boats aren't bringing danger?"

Shavore was shaking his head, and Dracut's heart dropped. The fact that he didn't trust the Ashen vanished at the simple gesture because his thoughts were on his wife. *Had the boats arrived? Was she still alive?*

"So they worship the sixth god then?"

Shavore nodded. "The god of chaos recreated Totailon's initial creation. But he made them just like him, chaotic. Most importantly, he made them stronger, more powerful. Unlike the goddess of peace who hides in the background but with control, he prefers to be right in the thick of everything, enjoying the chaos he brings."

"So my wife is battling against a race of humans who are stronger and chaotic?"

"Yes, but what should worry you more is that she is fighting against a god. Like I said, Magicot is not likely to just sit by and watch."

17

A Spy among Them

The sun had almost set behind the horizon, and yet the battle on the ocean's edge felt as if it had been moments before for many of the surviving soldiers. Despite the despair in the soldiers, none were in the same mental state as the surviving mage. Vixxen sat on a wagon's edge, changing the linen bandage wrapped around her wounded leg. The pain in her leg was bearable only because she was haunted by the sight of those soldiers killed by the deadly willow tree.

"You really should try to get some sleep." Vixxen looked up as a young combat mage with long blond hair came to sit beside her on the wagon. She'd never met the young mage prior to that day, but as the townspeople had fled down the path and into the forest, they had intercepted John and his twin brother Jine, and they had been good company to Vixxen for the majority of the afternoon.

"I tried," Vixxen said in honesty. It was true; she had lain down a couple times in an attempt to rest, knowing she would need her strength soon. But every time she closed her eyes, sleep was fleeting, finding ways to sneak up on her for a few minutes before the image of a deadly willow branch ripped the head off a young soldier's body. Sleep did not last long with such nightmares haunting her thoughts. It wasn't the death that was getting to the elite combat mage; no, death was always an expected thing in war. It was the new knowledge that she could have been the cause of the death of so many she was entrusted to protect that had stolen her spirit.

"You should try again," John said, obviously eyeing the cut on Vixxen's leg. "Just because the barbarians are content with taking over the town does not mean they will not pursue once enough of their boats have reached the shore and unloaded."

Vixxen had of course thought of this; it was for this reason exactly she had requested John and his brother stay with her toward the back of the fleeing townspeople—in case someone did come. At the moment, they were lacking in soldiers because most of those that had fled from the battle earlier that morning had rested quickly then joined the lord of Duerken and his captains in scoping out the town from the edge of the forest that bordered it. If the barbarians did pursue, it would be Vixxen, John, Jine, and just fewer than ten soldiers of Duerken that would stand between the pursuing killers and the many townspeople behind them.

This fact did not help Vixxen find sleep. The nightmares came anyway to awaken her, preventing her from preparing both her mind and her body for another battle. If there was any consolation at all, it was the idea that the longer they waited to pursue, the better chance reinforcements would arrive. She knew it could be days still before any of the combat mages that studied on the western coast of Frendilar would arrive, but she was letting herself hope Jaxxal would be successful with the Woodnips. The eastern Woodnips lived in the very forest they were passing through. They would be the first reinforcements to arrive, and Vixxen knew they were her best hope.

"That won't heal unless you sleep, and all of these people are counting on you to be at your best to protect them." Jine, John's twin brother, who was distinguishable from his brother only by the shorter cut of his hair, chimed in on Vixxen's lack of sleep as well. Vixxen turned to Jine then with the intent of repeating herself in anger—anger mostly with herself—but no words came for Jine was handing her a long white mage robe. It was hers of course; Jine had taken it from her to clean it. The white was symbolic among the mages and was only worn by the ten Tailles and the council leader. *Leader*, that's what it symbolized, and that's what these many people expected of her, and she was not ready to do that.

Vixxen let out a sigh, and instead of yelling at Jine, she chose to let her silence speak for her. He laid out her robe in her arms, and she knew that she must sleep, at least a little, or else her body would not be ready to fight off anyone.

"Fine," Vixxen said with a hint of defeat in her voice. "You promise to wake me if they signal."

"Immediately," Jine and John said together quickly. "And we will be ready to fight at your side this time."

Vixxen wasn't overly comfortable with the lord's decision to send a local thief into the town to spy. But the man had been company to the twin brothers, and they seemed content with trusting the young man named Hugheny. Vixxen had a bad feeling about it though, a bad feeling that had nothing to do with her inability to sleep. It was just like the feeling that told Vixxen the boats did not contain friendly beings, and her gut feelings were rarely wrong.

Hugheny had often sneaked through the streets of Duerken after dusk, but it had never been as difficult as it was this night. Shadows were difficult to find as there were so many fires—campfires for large groups of the barbaric warriors and larger fires burning down certain structures that obviously had been determined useless for the needs of these people.

He had a few important stops he had to make before reporting back, so he stuck to whatever shadows he could find.His black traveling cloak helped hide him from sight, and Hugheny was grateful that the barbarians did not seem to be expecting spies in their midst. They were enjoying themselves, cheering happily, singing songs. They were acting as though they'd won, and Hugheny understood why; they had been anchoring ships on the ocean all afternoon and had easily filled the town with their warriors. Many boats had not unloaded their men and women since so few could still fit in the town.

Hugheny didn't know how much these barbarians knew about the land they had attacked, but he doubted they could know all too much, because if they did, they would certainly not be celebrating. Yes, they took out many lives and emptied an entire town, but they weren't invading a town, they were invading a kingdom. A kingdom that was made up of three human kingdoms and two Woodnip tribes, and that was ignoring the mages. These barbarians couldn't win a war, Hugheny knew that, but the trick for Frendilar would be to reduce the damage inflicted onits inhabitants. Winning quicker and with fewer casualties was what both the mages and the lord of Duerken wanted to do.

Hugheny had volunteered to gather intel from within the town because he had often sneaked around the town both during the day and night. He had already informed the lord of Duerken of the anchoring boats and the fact that the barbarians were using the town as a sort of base for those that had gotten off the boats. As he reached the docks, the first thing he noticed was the lack of activity. There were no more barbarians rowing in small boats to shore from the anchored boats, and the fires that had been lit earlier in the day to burn the dead bodies had died. The giant willow tree had become extremely still, though it appeared the barbarians still kept their distance from it. This made spying on the goings-on of the beach much easier as the barbarians had avoided camping within distance of the once deadly willow tree.

It was a good start; Hugheny would now be able to make an honest estimation of the number of barbarians in town, knowing that at least for the time being, they had stopped bringing more in. He had already estimated that they had filled the town with more living bodies than had ever existed in the town at one time. This was not overly useful besides letting the Duerken soldiers know that they were definitely outnumbered.

Hugheny turned around, away from the docks and the shore. He started passing by different outdoor camps and taking peeks inside the houses that the barbarians had decided to camp out in. The most obvious thing Hugheny was able to recognize while sneaking around the town was that there was not a single child among the barbarians. Either they were still on the boats or this was not a conquest, but an assault. It did mean one positive thing to Hugheny; there was not a single innocent life in the town. They were all soldiers. This made collateral damage much less likely.

Nearly an hour passed quickly as Hugheny used the smoke from the fires and whatever shadows he could find to keep from being seen as he stealthily traveled among the barbarians. He was a little disappointed to notice that they were quite defensive. Very few were sleeping at any given time, and almost all of them were actually sleeping with their weapons still sheathed at their side. Hugheny wondered if they expected to be attacked in their sleep by the soldiers of Frendilar or by each other. They seemed a bit too comfortable sleeping with their weapons for it to be a new thing to them. How could anyone live like that, so untrusting of those around them? Hugheny was a thief and a black-market trader and even he trusted most people. He never once feared to be attacked in his sleep. These barbarians were both brutal and paranoid. Could that be used against them?

It was getting late, and Hugheny knew he needed to report back soon, but he didn't quite have the estimate he was trying to get of the army's size. It was large; he was beginning to think that nearly five thousand barbarian warriors were within the town walls. The Duerken soldiers were down to under two hundred men and women soldiers, and they were spread out among the forest border attempting to gather information from a safe distance. So with that number in mind, Hugheny began inching toward the secret exit he'd used in the northern part of the town wall. He was not expecting anyone to be in that small back alley that was used to bury bones from the local butcher, but a young woman was leaning against the wall in the alley.

"Hello," the woman said to him sweetly. "Took you a while to come back this time. I thought perhaps you'd snuck out a different way." Hugheny could not quite make out the woman's features in the dark, just her silhouette.She was tall, probably just under six feet, but she seemed rather short to be a barbarian as they all seemed to tower around seven feet. Was she a spy like him, sent in for information?He knew there were a couple other volunteers, but he hadn't run into any.

"I believe it's polite to return my greeting," the woman said, coaxing a response from him.

"I don't know you," Hugheny said, deciding that, in the middle of war, pleasantries were unnecessary. He quickly recognized his mistake as she stepped into the light given off by one of the large building fires in the background. She was short for a barbarian, but her outfit and rough, scarred skin told him that she was certainly not human. She was dressed in a crude leather-hide outfit that had obviously been cut and designed by someone who had not had a lot of practice in making clothing. He had missed this in the dark because she did have on a dark traveler's cloak over it, most likely taken from a home here in Duerken.

"You seem a bit short in comparison to the rest of your people," Hugheny said, attempting to buy time as his mind started counting the many hidden knives stored on his body. The long wooden staff she held would have seemed a lot less intimidating if it wasn't for the long crescent-shaped blade that jutted out the top of it, curving down half the stick.

"Yes," said the barbarian woman. "I am quite short, but I survive because what I lack in strength and stature I make up for in intelligence. There isn't a smarter member of the Xile Tribe." Hugheny made a quick note of that. Perhaps he could gain some information from the woman if he could keep her talking.

Hugheny barely had time to react as the thought of keeping her talking had relaxed his defenses, and so when she charged at him, he only just managed to duck underneath her crescent-headed ax. He managed to unsheathe two daggers from behind his pants, but he wasn't quite sure what he could do with such small weapons against such a deadly enemy. Normally, such weapons were at a disadvantage against Hugheny because they were slow, but this long weapon did not appear to be all too heavy, and the barbarian moved it so quickly he knew speed would not be on his side. So instead of trying to get in close enough to stab his enemy, he began throwing his daggers at her, aiming for vital points on the barbarian's body.

The daggers traveled quick and true, but the woman managed to sidestep one and deflect another with the wooden part of her staff. She was an agile warrior, perhaps the only agile barbarian he had seen the entire day. He quickly unsheathed two more, backing up away from the barbarian while letting them fly in her direction. She dodged another and then reached up and caught the fourth one. He turned around, preparing to flee east in the shadows, hoping he could lose her and find another way to sneak out of the city. But he wouldn't get a chance for the barbarian was too quick. He supposed he should be thankful that she hit him in the head with the blunt portion of her weapon instead of the long crescent blade, but as he fell to the ground, nearly unconscious, he realized he would be a prisoner of war. The mere thought made him wonder if death would not have been a better choice.

"I like you," he heard the woman say. Her voice seemed far away, and he knew that the hit he took to the back of his head was quickly delivering him into unconsciousness. "You don't rely on brute strength. You're more like me. But you will need to be questioned, of course. My brother will want to see what he can learn from you. You see, my brother is the leader of the Xile Tribe. Despite my interest in you, I cannot deny him the chance to learn."

THE TRUE BRAINS OF THE XILE

When Hugheny came back to consciousness, he was unable to see a thing—not because of some kind of damage to his eyes but because he was blindfolded. He could not feel a breeze chilling his body, so he assumed he was indoors, but where exactly was beyond his abilities of deduction. His hands were bound with some very thick rope. He started thinking of many similar situations he had been in over the years, but no smile came to his lips this time as he attempted to test the knot that bound his hands together. He remembered the barbarian that had probably tied them; she had mentioned being the smartest of her entire race, and he quickly realized that his fears were true. The knot in the rope was very well tied, and it was very unlikely that he'd be able to wiggle free.

He began to try and stand but realized his legs were bound together too. So he did the only thing he was still capable of, he rolled to his right and was glad to feel many of his knives and daggers still concealed within his cloak and cloth garments. Perhaps the barbarian had assumed he'd used them all, or she didn't think he could get to them as long as he was tied up. Either way, it was a bit comforting to know he was still armed. He rolled a bit more, trying to get a dagger to loosen from its sheath so that he could try to cut the rope with it. As he rolled about, he felt his knee hit solid wood, and he quickly realized he'd probably gotten close to the door to the room for he could hear voices. He stopped rolling and focused on his breathing, reducing his intake and release of air to small, quiet breaths, making it possible to make out the words in the other room.

"It's the way of our people.As both our leader and my brother, you can't deny me this." Hugheny recognized that voice; it belonged to the barbaric woman who had knocked him out. The other voice belonged to a guy, her brother, obviously. It was a bit deep, and Hugheny pictured a very large, muscular barbarian to own such a deep voice.

"He's an enemy," the deep voice said. "We are at war."

"And you don't think I don't know this? I know what he is. I have done my part in bringing him to you so you can learn what you can from him about our enemies. That does not change the fact that I defeated him."

"And that was difficult?"

"Our customs don't require it be difficult, just that it was done. He is mine to do with as I please. You may question him, but you may not kill him."

"And I must return him to you when I'm done."

"You think I'd leave such a valuable prize with you, brother?" There was a deep sinister laugh that followed that statement, and Hugheny felt his stomach vanish. They were discussing his fate, and he didn't quite like the idea of being questioned by any man that a voice so deadly could belong to, let alone one of these ruthless barbarians.

"You think I'll risk losing this war over something as small as our customs on a man's life?"

"I won't bother reminding you that I don't share your optimism in a possible victory."

"Magicot—"

"Oh right, the all-seeing and powerful shaman says you can win. However did I forget?" Hugheny wanted to laugh at the obvious sarcasm present in the barbarian's voice. It was obvious to Hugheny that she did not share her brother's views on this Magicot. "Ah, yes, what is it you believe he is again? Let me see, oh yes, you seem to be under the misconception that he is some god."

"It's more likely than the fact that he has been constantly reincarnated every time he has died."

"Well, if he is such a god, then we can't lose."

"I told you, he doesn't care if we win or lose. He just wants to see us fight. Is it so hard to believe that he doesn't care about us? He wants to mix things up. We've been here for how long, less than a day? And you've already lost many men including your own son." Hugheny could hear himself breathing now. Silence had fallen on the other side of the door, and his breathing was all that was possible to hear. It was quite some time before there were words again between the barbarian siblings.

"I'm sorry," the woman said.

"Forget it." The brother's voice sounded weaker and no longer held that command it had held so recently. "Bring him out. I'll question him, and if he tells me what I need to hear, then he's all yours." Hugheny wanted to hear the woman argue, but all he heard were footsteps, and he recognized the addition of light into the room even through the blindfold that was wrapped tightly around his eyes.

A strong hand lifted him off the ground and dragged him across the floor. When they dropped him down, he felt himself lifted into a kneeling position; and as the blindfold was removed from his eyes, he felt all the color in his face drain away. The woman's brother was scarier than he had pictured. He towered over Hugheny, over seven feet high. He was dressed in leather armor like the rest of the barbarians, but despite it using more material, it seemed to cover less. The muscles on this barbarian were huge, unlike anything he had ever seen before, and sheathed on his back were two swords with blades that just may have been longer than Hugheny himself was tall.

"Well, you don't appear to be much of a soldier." Hugheny shook his head and felt his whole body shudder as the barbarian let out a deep laugh. "Well then, spy. My sister here seems to have plans for your life, so let's try to keep you alive. I only have a couple questions. Answer me truthfully, and I'll give you over to her without a scratch."

Hugheny watched as the barbarian unsheathed one of those monster swords, and the need to survive took over. He had no intention of lying to this giant, but that didn't mean that he'd be allowed to live.

"By the look in your eyes, I feel I may just get the truth out of you. So let's start with a simple one. Where did the giant tree come from?"

Hugheny had to take a deep breath and spit into his own mouth before he was actually able to respond. It was only then that he realized how dry his mouth had become. "The, um, mage, um, died." There was a puzzled look on the barbarian, and Hugheny knew he would need to get his nerves in check if he was going to survive. He took a deeper breath. "A mage died in combat. Some of the more experienced mages build up magic in their bodies in case of emergencies. If it isn't released while they are alive, when they die, it is released in unpredictable ways."

"And do you know the mage I killed?"

Hugheny wanted to be surprised to hear that this barbarian had been the one to kill Vixxen's colleague, but he wasn't. "Knew of him."

"Was he powerful?"

"Yes. He was one of ten Taille mages. They are the elite combat specialists."

"There are ten as powerful as him?" This seemed to trouble the large barbarian leader, and Hugheny was glad to see that the monster of a man could be troubled. This made him appear just a bit weaker and less powerful to Hugheny, although when the brother turned to him awaiting a response, that apparent weakness vanished.

"At least as powerful. I have met a Taille mage who fights with swords of wind and moves like it as well."

The barbarian didn't seem interested in learning more about the other Tailles. His interest appeared focused on the two he had already met. "And the woman mage?"

"Yes, she is a Taille."

"Are the others coming?"

"I honestly don't know. We sent for them, but there is no way to know how long it could take."

The barbarian leader began to pace the room, and Hugheny found himself looking around inside one of the larger of the town's market stores. Obviously, this barbarian had chosen it for the size of this very room, and Hugheny couldn't deny that it was a good choice for a leader's main sitting area. The sister was standing against the wall, and it was quite apparent she was attempting to appear taller than she truly was. Hugheny recognized that she stood straight and rigid, not leaning or slumping in the slightest. He expected this was customary for her and possibly any barbarian as short as she was. He had a strange feeling that these beings did not respect anything that made them appear weak.

"Just one more question, and you can have the pitiful thing," the barbarian addressed his sister then, and Hugheny watched as she nodded in delight. "Where is this woman mage?"

Hugheny was afraid of this question. He wanted to lie but knew it would be too dangerous for him to do so, and knowing that he just needed to answer this question to survive forced the truth from his lips. He told the barbarian leader all about the fleeing townspeople and the fact that Vixxen was following them closely so as to defend them from pursuers.

"How many of your soldiers are with her?"

Hugheny knew that he had to lie about this, and when he muttered out "none," he knew he had convinced the barbarian that he had not wanted to tell him this. A large smile appeared on the barbarian's face, and Hugheny was quickly worried about Vixxen.He could only hope that Jine and John could protect her from whatever came her way because of him.

The barbarian was still smiling when he turned his attention to his sister. "Let's give your god a second chance."

"Are you making fun of me?"

"Of course," the brother said, still smiling. "Take your puny prize and have someone fetch me my shaman." It was strange to watch the sister give the most fake bow Hugheny had ever seen before she picked him up by the ropes binding his hand and dragged him out into the center of the town.

Hugheny was too distracted by his own despicable actions of betrayal to pay any attention to his surroundings. He assumed the woman had mentioned this shaman to one of the guards positioned outside the leader's chosen base, but he couldn't be sure. When he finally did focus on his location, he was back in the dark alley with the many buried bones—the very same alley he'd first run into the barbarian woman, and he was a little shocked to find she had released his bindings.

"Congratulations, you get to survive," the woman said.

"You're letting me go?"

"I told you, I like you."

To Hugheny, this seemed a strange thing to say to an enemy. "I can just leave?" She just nodded, and Hugheny was waiting for her to attack him again. But she didn't. "Why?"

She chuckled slightly, and it was only then that Hugheny truly noticed how unlike the other barbaric women she was, not just in stature, but despite her fitness, she wasn't as muscular either. She was actually quite pretty, and he realized only then that she could truly pass as a human if it wasn't for her garments. She had very long black hair that had been hiding within the traveling cloak, and she had a very young look upon her. She was definitely younger than Hugheny. Was it possible that this was sincere and not a trap?

"I know this must be difficult to grasp, but I'm not tricking you. I should like to know your name though."

"Hugheny." He didn't know why he said it so casually, as if he wasn't in pure confusion of the situation he had found himself. It wasn't a rushed answer despite how badly he just wanted to disappear from this location and find someone who could warn Vixxen that they would be coming for her.

"Effauna is my name," she said. "And unlike so many of these idiots, I can see that we don't stand a chance in winning a war here. This was just one town, and I know we'll lose. Maybe not tomorrow, but sooner or later, we will not be the victors in this war."

"And so you've chosen to help speed it along by letting me live?"

"Not quite. I've spared your life, but I do ask for something in return." There it was. Hugheny knew it was too simple. What could she want? He didn't have to ask though for she pointed Hugheny to the exit of the town and added, "I simply ask that when it's the other way around, you repay the favor. I'm giving you your life, and in return, I expect you to give me mine."

TRAVELING THROUGH HATRED

Vixxen knew she had actually managed to sleep for a while because when she awoke, it was dark, and by the look of it, it was deep into the night. Vixxen was bothered for the screaming and scrambling sounds from her nightmare had not diminished when she awoke. She quickly noticed that her ride had stopped, and the villagers in front of her on the path were yelling and attempting to create a distance between the mages and themselves.

"Hate to be a bother, Vixxen," said Jine, who was standing above her, "but we are about to have company." Vixxen bolted upright, her runic rod was in her hand before she was standing straight, and she knew why the twins had awoken her. Down the path a ways, it was possible to hear footsteps and make out a light, most likely from many torches. It sounded like a procession. The barbarians were coming.

"I'm a little surprised they pursued tonight, to be honest," Vixxen said. "The soldiers said they appeared to be focused on getting as many of their warriors as they could off the boats and on land."

"It doesn't sound like a whole lot of them either," John said. "Listen, maybe a dozen or so footsteps."

"Think they knew how few of us were on the backline?" Jine asked.

"That might actually explain it," said Vixxen. "If they managed to capture any of the spies the lord of Duerken was sending in the town, they may have been able to learn that there were only a few of us protecting the back end of the caravan." The footsteps were getting closer, and once they turned the corner and saw that they had come upon their enemies, Vixxen knew she would be fighting again very soon.

The twins gasped in unison as the barbarians turned the corner, and Vixxen understood why. It was as if they had handpicked the largest of their warriors to come after them.All twelve barbarians were over seven feet tall and nothing but muscle—all but the man leading them,the barbarian Vixxen had fought earlier, the one with magic. It was then that she recognized the fact that they were not carrying torches but that the magical barbarian was actually carrying fire itself.

"Lights on, boys," Vixxen said casually as she focused her magic on her runic rod. It immediately burned with bright red fire, becoming her long deadly spear of flames. It gave off an immense amount of light that fell onto the dark path of the forest, and beside her, John's and Jine's large burning swords were lit as well. The flames danced in preparation for battle, and Vixxen had to quickly second-guess her decision not to try shooting flaming arrows first, but she somehow knew they weren't coming for the caravan with such a small force. They were coming for her.

"The smaller one is mine," Vixxen said. It was clear she was giving an order, but both John and Jine laughed casually as if the order was some kind of joke.

"Sure, let the Taille take the only non-giant coming," said Jine.

"None of them are giants," said Vixxen. "I know. I've met a giant. Besides, I'm doing you both a favor.The smaller one is the only one I've met so far capable of magic."

"All yours then," said John with a smile. Vixxen had to shake her head. The two men beside her were trained in combat but were very young, and they were treating this threat like nothing more than a training exercise. She felt both relaxed and afraid at the same time for she couldn't expect them to have ever been in combat outside of a training exercise. Perhaps it was good they were treating it as such.

She wasn't sure and just had to trust in them to distract and combat the other barbarians while she focused on the magical one.

It happened quickly. The fire in the hands of the barbarian vanished, and they charged forward. John and Jine joined in the charge, only allowing the magical barbarian to pass, and before he reached Vixxen, she had to smile as the ten soldiers remaining behind emerged from the trees to join in the fight against the barbarians. The barbarians were obviously surprised by the even numbers, and that gave Vixxen a confidence as her spear of fire raised up to parry the incoming spear aimed at her head.

"Interesting," said the barbarian. "Was only supposed to be you guarding the path."

Vixxen's smile did not fade away. "Guess you shouldn't trust your sources." It was the only spoken words as Vixxen tried to turn her spear over to push the barbarian off balance with the distraction of the conversation, but it was obvious he had been expecting such a maneuver. He remained in perfect form, turning his own spear over to parry and then taking another swing at Vixxen's head. She ducked below it easily, but the sudden force placed on her legs reminded her that she was still not 100 percent from her earlier injury. She tried to ignore the pain as she jabbed her spear at an upward angle, expecting to at least catch him in the side a little but was quickly disappointed when the spear collided with a magical barrier.

The barbarian backed up a bit, putting himself quite a bit out of reach of her fiery spear; he seemed to really be interested in having a conversation with her. This was difficult for Vixxen though as she could see that although John and Jine were holding their own against the barbarians farther down the path, the same could not be said about the Duerken soldiers. It looked as though almost all of them were dead or injured, and only a couple of barbarians had been taken out of the fight. John and Jine were buying time with their fiery swords of death, and it appeared to Vixxen that the magical barbarian may just be trying to buy time for the rest of his men to get by them and to his aid in cutting her down.

"I remember the mages being much better fighters the last time I was in this land," the barbarian said. Vixxen felt a small amount of anger surface at the obvious insult. Was that his plan, to blind her with anger using insults? "A hundred years of peace have not been kind to you."

Vixxen raised her spear in front of her, but it wasn't in some sort of salute or surrender. She quickly grabbed at thin air behind the spear, and the flames bent, shaping into her fiery bow so quickly she doubted the barbarian would be able to react to the release of her fiery arrow. How wrong she was as she watched the flames explode into another magical barrier she could not see. That was a trick she knew she'd have to learn if she got out of this war alive.

◆◆◆◆◆

Dracut should not have known his wife was in danger. She was on the opposite corner of the kingdom, and he was deep in the center of a mountain. But it turned out that Shavore's younger sister was not only able to see into the future on occasion, but she had the powerful ability to see the present anywhere she wanted to. When Dracut found it impossible to do anything but worry about his wife, Shavore had had her look out across the kingdom in hopes of putting him at peace, but they had learned how much danger she was in.

"She is fighting a Xile with magic," Shavore said a little too calmly. Dracut had been listening to Shavore recount to him what his little sister had seen for some time, but Dracut's patience had grown extremely thin.

"Yes," Dracut said angrily. "She is caught in hand-to-hand combat with a god, and I couldn't possibly be farther away." His large muscles gave way as he slammed his fist into the rock wall of the mountain. The wall shook slightly, and many small rocks fell from the ceiling above. If Dracut had been able to notice anything beyond his own fears, he may have noticed a look of delight on the Ashen's face at his outburst. As it was, he noticed nothing, and Dracut felt no pain in his hand but avoided swinging at the wall in anger in fear of burying himself alive in such a horridly dreary place.

"It is a predicament," said Shavore, again with too much calm. The calmness in the Ashen just added to the rage and fear welling up inside of Dracut. How could someone be so calm; there was absolutely nothing anyone could do for his wife, and yet they were supposed to somehow remain calm with the knowledge that the council had placed him so far away, so unable to help. "But perhaps a predicament we can get around."

Dracut turned on the Ashen very quickly, still with quite a bit of unabated rage. "My wife was the only mage in the entire council tower ever able to teleport beyond a few feet, and the few times she did it, she had to sleep for days to get her strength back."

"That's because teleporting is unnatural. Even the gods couldn't do it regularly," the calm Ashen said, traveling across the dark and damp cave. "But dark magic can take advantage of such unnatural powers. Such as with this."

Dracut only stared at the wall where the Ashen pointed. "It's just a symbol," Dracut said. "An upside-down heart with an *X* through it.It was the symbol of your kind."

"Oh, you mages know so little." Shavore almost appeared to smile at the knowledge that Dracut yet again knew so little about his kind. "It's not a symbol, it's a rune. Like the backward 3 on your robes."

"The Taille rune?"

"Exactly, the language of the gods."

Dracut looked down at his robes, at the large black backward 3 with the line straight through it. He had always known it was a rune, a powerful word written in the language of the gods. It hadn't ever occurred to him that the Ashen symbol was a rune as well. "But what does that matter?" Dracut was still very angry at the apparent stall.

"Runes are magical if you know how to use them. Come here and put your hand on it."

Dracut was a bit hesitant as he walked across the cave and slowly placed his hand on the rune in the wall. He didn't know how to work it though. "Well, what am I supposed to do?"

"You want to save your wife?"

Dracut gave Shavore an extremely deadly look at these words, as if the simple fact that he wanted to save his wife should have been enough to make the rune work.

"I apologize I'm wasting your time. This rune is our symbol because it's the symbol of our god. It means hate, and you have to truly fill your entire mind and body with hate in order to make it work. But when you do, it can get you where you want to go."

"But hate is evil. I don't hate anyone."

"Hate is *not* evil," Shavore said angrily. "That is an extreme misconception. Hatred is an emotion, a form of dislike at the highest level. No different than love as the highest level of like. If you are capable of love, then you are also capable of hate."

Vixxen was feeling weaker with each parry, with each swing of her fiery spear, and she was only finding comfort in the fact that John and Jine had managed to construct a type of fiery wall with their swords, holding the other barbarians at bay, keeping them from passing in order to join the fight against her. She didn't think it mattered though. This magical barbarian did not need anyone's help. He didn't seem to be tired or even hurt, and as she again managed to block an incoming swing of his spear with her own, a recent wound in her arm sent another shudder of pain through her entire upper body. Her older leg wound gave way, and her next swing—meant only to defensively put her back on balance—collided expectantly with an invisible magical barrier.

Vixen was losing the battle, and she didn't think she could hold on much longer. If anything about her situation showed her how certain she was that she was losing, it was that her mind stopped focusing on the battle, stopped focusing on trying to stay alive, and instead spread to the thought of her daughter, to the sole idea that she may never get to meet the young woman she would grow up into.

Perhaps it was instinct or a mother's will to survive, but she found strength enough to parry another swing of the barbarian's spear, and suddenly, she had managed to gain her balance once again; and when she jabbed forward with her fiery spear in retaliation, she didn't relent, jabbing toward her opponent again and again. Each jab of her fiery spear collided with a magical barrier, but she was certain each one would, and she put extra magic behind each jab of her spear, causing each barrier to collapse on impact. It was a battle of power now. Who had the power and the will to keep it up, Vixxen with her relentless jabs, or the barbarian with his constant summoning of almost pitiful magical barriers.

Perhaps the ease at which the barriers fell apart should have been the true warning to Vixxen, but she was focused on survival and didn't recognize the bait until it was too late. A strong jab collided with nothing, and since the consistent collision had created a rhythm in her motions, the lack of a collision unbalanced the skilled and deadly mage. It was all the change in pace the barbarian needed as he retaliated with a jab of his own. The pain was fleeting because that deadly spear punctured a large hole right through Vixxen's heart, and she was dead before her brain could register that she was in any sort of pain.

"Who do you hate?" Shavore shouted at Dracut.

"I told you I don't hate anyone."

"Your wife may already be dead!" Shavore shouted. "And if that's the case, whose fault would that be?"

"That god," Dracut said angrily.

"Do you really feel like it's his fault? Is it his fault you aren't there to protect her? Is it your fault that no mage is there to help her?"

"The council," Dracut said quietly. "It's their fault I'm not there."

"So if she's dead, and you could have saved her?"

"She's not dead!" Dracut screamed. He could feel his hand start to burn and sweat as it put pressure on the stone wall, the carved shape of the rune felt along the palm of his hand.

"She's fighting a god. Who is there to save her?"

"No one," Dracut said, quietly again. It was true; there was no one there to save her. Not a single soul there to protect her from this god of chaos.

"Then she's dead."

"No!" It was quick, but it was indeed a painful experience. The rune his hand was on began to burn in purple dragon flames, and quickly, it carried to his hand. Fear showed in Dracut's eyes as the purple flames quickly engulfed his entire body. It burned, and Dracut could hear himself screaming, and then the pain vanished. He was standing on a path in a forest, staring at a battle between two black-robed mages with large fiery swords and about half a dozen warriors simply clad in leather who were even larger in muscle than Dracut himself. There was no denying that they were strong and powerful, but their muscles would prove to be useless weapons for defending themselves, for lying at Dracut's feet was his wife, and the hole in her chest through her heart left a hole in his heart, and every last one of them were going to pay for creating that hole.

20

REVENGE OF A TAILLE

Dracut could not possibly know what had happened to his wife. He had no way of knowing who had killed her, but he did have a pretty damn good idea of who his enemies were, and that was all that mattered then. He had failed to save his wife, and he knew deep in his heart that it was because he was too slow to hate, and he was never going to make the same mistake again. He charged forward, quickly passing the two black-robed mages and moved directly into the middle of the commotion.

Despite the full foot advantage the barbarians held over Dracut, it was them that showed fear in their eyes at his daring for when his maces burned to life in his hands, they took on a life of their own. Unlike his usual bright red fiery maces, these weapons were made up of the dark purple flames of a dragon's breath, and the barbarians had every right to fear those deadly magical weapons. As the first barbarian attempted to use his large wooden club to parry them, their collision caused an explosion of purple flames. A scream unlike anything Dracut had ever heard before filled the air as the barbarian dropped to the ground, grabbing his arm where the purple flames were melting away the flesh and muscle as if theywere nothing but paper.

As one barbarian lay screaming on the ground, three more charged in; and despite their unnatural strength, they were of no match for the deadly mage that was Dracut. As little thought existed in his mind, he had no trouble fighting on pure hatred and instinct as those deadly maces collided with swords and spears alike. If the barbarians thought they could brute-force their way past those deadly weapons, they were gravely mistaken for Dracut's muscles matched them almost evenly, and all any of their attacks managed to do was create more explosions of purple fire.

More screams of pain wrenched into the air as another barbarian fell to the ground, actually writhing in pain as the skin and flesh of his stomach melted away. Dracut was now fighting two-against-one, and the odds were greatly in his favor. The two barbarians attempted to work together, both coming in high with their large swords of steel, but Dracut just swung both his maces in a mix of offensive and defensive maneuvers, and both barbarians had a minute to regret swinging in high as the explosions of dragon's breath quickly melted their faces straight to their skulls.

With four barbarians dead or dying on the ground, the two remaining ones fighting the young combat mages tried to turn to the woods and flee, but as their attention had turned to fleeing from Dracut, they were punished for their fear with large fiery swords through the chest. As they burned up into ash in front of Dracut's eyes, his mind began to focus on his surroundings for the first time. There was no remaining enemy to fight, and the anger and hatred, although far from abated, began to subside from his outer appearance, and he found himself looking into the faces of friends.

John and Jine had once been pupils of his, and he only then recognized how many lay dead around him at his feet. Nearly two dozen dead bodies lay on the path between the trees or within the trees themselves. In numbers, the battle had been quite even as far as he could tell, but the Xile, as Shavore had called them, had obviously outmatched the Duerken soldiers, and only John and Jine had been able to stand their ground against such a deadly foe.

"Dracut," John said then in the softest whisper of pain and sorrow Dracut thought he had ever heard. He remembered when the twins had come to the tower to begin their training with a knack for fighting. He had been a mentor, and in return, they had been his friends, and he knew his pain was their pain. He placed a hand on John's shoulder as he passed by them to his wife's body. It was more painful than he could have ever imagined, and his strong outer shell broke as tears flooded his face. He bent down and lifted her head, trying his best to ignore the large gaping hole where her heart belonged as he hugged her and cried.

Magicot watched from the trees as the large and powerful Taille mage suddenly appeared on the path in a burst of dragon's fire. It had been a specialty of his old friend Haidier, the god of hate. As god of chaos, Magicot knew that if Haidier was helping the mages, then the god was getting something in return. But then Magicot had no way of knowing whether it had been Haidier's own magic or if the mage had found some other way to use the teleport magic of hate and dragon's fire. Magicot knew all too well that mages had the ability to tap into the power of the gods—for Magicot himself had given those abilities to the first of the dark mages himself.

He didn't dwell too long on his old friend or his old powers though as the mage charged into the battle with the remaining Xile and, in mere minutes, tore them apart with deadly maces of dragon's fire. There was a smile on Magicot's face through the entire massacre of his people for there was no plan of action anywhere in the combat. The mage fought in a pure and chaotic way, and it created confusion and chaos among the Xiles as well. It was truly a sight to behold, and Magicot had a front-row seat to the bloodbath.

His enjoyment and happiness were fleeting though as he recognized the pain in the mage's face. If there was one thing Magicot fancied over chaos, it was survival. He knew even before the powerful Taille mage lifted the head of the one he himself had killed, and began to cry, that Magicot himself would be that mage's true target of revenge.

When Magicot had decided to take on Deerskyn's mission to finish off the remaining Taille mage, he thought it might extend the time of the war by reducing Frendilar's current defenses; but if he had known that he would be making an enemy of a mage that he knew he didn't stand a chance against in combat, then he would have left her alive. Survival was now Magicot's only concern because what was the point in creating a chaotic war between two completely different groups of people if hecouldn't be around to witness it?

———◦◆◦◦◆◦———

It was a while before Dracut rested his wife's head down on the dirt path, and he felt the tender and comforting touch of two friends' hands on his shoulders. He sniffled back the remaining tears and then allowed his anger and hatred to begin to resurface.

"Which one killed her?" Dracut asked with a deep and raspy voice, a little unlike his normal voice.

"The one with magic," John answered sternly.

"He must have run for it when you arrived," Jine added quickly. Dracut stood up and looked around. The only Xile to have magic was the god, just as Shavore had told him. Dracut quickly wished he hadn't been so reserved in trusting the Ashen; perhaps if he had been a bit more trusting, he would have arrived in time.

"The woods!" John shouted, pointing at a spot within the trees that had very recently been disturbed. A large and heavy footprint showed that Magicot had indeed run into the forest to escape after murdering his wife, and Dracut's hatred was now boiling forward again as instinct drove him forward into the forest without a second thought.

"Keep her safe!" he shouted back at the twins. He didn't turn around to see if they had heard him, and the shout that reached him in response did not register with his mind as his one focus drove him forward. His focus became lacking in common sense for he knew nothing about Magicot besides the fact that he was a god. That knowledge should have been enough to put Dracut on the defensive, but he didn't recognize that this could result in his own death for he truly didn't care if it did or not. He was going to find this god, and he was going to make him pay for the death of his wife.

Soon instinct began to show it had a weakness as Dracut began to realize that he was following a god that could be nearly an hour ahead of him, not to mention it was still the middle of the night, and the moonlight was not very visible through the thick foliage and trees of the forest. He knew in the back of his head that he needed to slow down long enough to get his bearings, but he continued to plow forward into the forest, following a path he himself felt he would take if he had run from a battle, not that he would ever do so.

The maces emitted purple light from their flames, but it was all the light Dracut had to use. A feeling deep in his gut told him he was going the right way, told him he was closing the gap between him and his foe, and there was no way for Dracut to know how right he was until he plowed into a small clearing. Here, the trees and ground spread out enough to allow for a bit of moonlight, and standing in the middle of the clearing under the moonlight, waiting for him, was unmistakably a Xile.

"Are you Magicot?" Dracut asked forcefully, prepared to charge and kill no matter the answer. He only asked the question in hopes he could be sure he was indeed killing his wife's murderer.

"Ah, you know of me. Do you know what I am then?"

"You're a murder!" Dracut yelled.

"I'm a god." There was a force with this statement, but it may have been whispered for Dracut knew already and didn't quite care.

Dracut charged forward. "Then let's find out if a god can die." Dracut had hoped to catch Magicot off guard, but the god had been ready for his lunge and simply ducked below the dragon's fire and then, without ever retaliating, turned and ran back into the forest. Anger and hatred fueled Dracut as he ran after the murdering god.

"Fight me like a man!" Dracut yelled after the fleeing god, but his words seemed to do nothing to deter the fleeing Xile. Dracut soon found himself fighting the forest instead of the murdering god. He was bashing large branches out of his way and completely trampling over thorn bushes and other wildlife, but all of these distractions seemed inconsequential to his foe. Magicot jumped over bushes of thorns and completely ignored all manner of obstacles as if they didn't exist at all.

It was obvious to Dracut that he himself was faster than Magicot, but Magicot continued to dodge and jump the forest obstacles almost as if they didn't exist at all, and it was only this very fact that kept the distance between the hunter and the hunted. And as hours passed, Dracut's legs screamed in pain, asking him to break, and it was only his pure desire for revenge that managed to keep pushing him forward.He was soon rewarded for his determination for Magicot had stopped in front of a tree that had a trunk wider than a castle tower and seemed to stretch nearly as tall. Dracut had finally caught his foe.

"Nowhere left to run," Dracut said with a smile. His legs were physically exhausted, but it didn't matter because it was his mentality that was keeping him strong and deadly. Magicot just looked at him with a grin upon his face as if taunting him to attack. Dracut gladly accepted the god's challenge, and he repeated his earlier lunge forward, this time swinging lower, expecting his enemy to try and duck below the swing as he'd done before. But Dracut was not rewarded with a collision to flesh but instead found his deadly maces taking out entire chunks of the large tree.

He looked around and his enemy was gone and he could not figure out where he had gone. Dracut could not remember Magicot ducking or sidestepping or even moving at all, and all logic told Dracut that he should have made contact with his enemy,should have burned him alive where he had stood.And only then did reason begin to sink into his thick skull. He had been fooled hours ago; he hadn't been chasing Magicot, but a magical copy meant to lead him away. His pure desire for revenge had been the thing to deny it from him, and he began slamming the fiery maces into the large tree in front of him in anger. Entire chunks of the tree flew across the forest with every swing, and Dracut did not relent. His anger and hatred fueled swing after swing into the giant tree, and he didn't tire, didn't lose momentum until his mental exhaustion matched his physical exhaustion. He found himself leaning against the beaten tree among the rubble that remained of its original stature, and Dracut felt like the tree. He finally felt truly defeated.

21

A JEWELED DAGGER

It didn't seem to matter that morning was beginning to get closer for the forest seemed to get darker as the moon vanished from the sky above before the sun had begun to rise. Hugheny and Jahkan were having trouble traveling through the woods in the dark, and Hugheny knew they would never reach Vixxen in time to warn her about what he expected may be coming for her, but he refused to give up.

"Careful there," Jahkan said, pointing to a large thorny bush. "Those can be poisonous sometimes." Hugheny came to an immediate stop but was only frustrated as he found himself having to detour around yet another obstacle.

"I've done a lot of wrong," Hugheny said, finally venting his frustration to the young captain. "But this is the first time I feel guilty. It will be the first time someone loses their life because of my selfishness."

"You survived," Jahkan said in an attempt to comfort him, "and all you did was tell them a mage was alone on the path, which wasn't even a true statement. You lied and told enough of the truth to get out of there alive yourself. There isn't a soul alive who would blame you."

"I'd blame me," Hugheny said with a long, deep sigh.

"Then don't. You have just as much right to try to live as anyone else. You were captured, tied up, and you saw one way to live. Vixxen is one of the most powerful mages in Frendilar, and she was protected by ten of our own soldiers and two combat mages who were trained by Dracut." It was all true, but Hugheny could not shake the feeling that it wouldn't matter.

"I'll feel better if we can get to her," Hugheny began to respond, but he noticed Jahkan had stopped walking and was doing his best to signal Hugheny to be quiet and to stand still. Once Hugheny did as Jahkan wanted, he could hear it too. Someone else was in the forest and moving very quickly, and they were moving right toward them. Hugheny slowly but quietly drew two long daggers out from inside his cloak and noticed that without hearing him do so, Jahkan had unsheathed his sword as well. Hugheny hoped for only a second that the coming footsteps did not belong to an enemy and that there would be no need to fight, no need to delay. That second passed quickly as the running man came into view, and even in the dark, there was no mistaking the man's choice in clothing.

Jahkan jumped the running Xile barbarian the minute he was in range and somehow managed to avoid spearing himself on the enemy's long spear. The barbarian was obviously taken by surprise because Jahkan very easily managed to cut a long, gaping gash in his cheek with his sword, but after that, it was clear to Hugheny that the barbarian had the upper hand in combat, and that worried Hugheny because if he would have expected anyone to be able to go toe to toe in combat with a Xile, it would have been Captain of the Guard, Jahkan Yute.

———————◆◆◆◆◆———————

Magicot could feel the deep gash in his cheek, and he found himself a little bit humbled when he realized the wound had been given to him by a mere soldier and not a powerful mage. As he parried another swing from the soldier's sword, that humbleness turned to embarrassment. Sure, the soldier was a decent fighter, but it was obvious that without magic, he could not hope to best Magicot, god of chaos, in a one-on-one fight; and the only reason he had been able to surprise him was because of how afraid he had been of the pursuing mage.

He had run headlong into the woods, never looking back after the mage had taken his bait and chased the illusion. He could not be sure of how long that chase would go on.For all he knew, the mage had figured the ruse quickly and turned and was nearly minutes on his heel, and with that possibility etched into his head, he recognized how dangerous this new distraction was. Here, he was fighting a simple soldier, allowing the deadly mage to make up the ground he hoped his illusion had created.

Magicot tried to take the offensive to, at minimum, put the soldier at bay enough for him to continue to run, but the soldier was intelligent and had recognized that he was losing and, thus, had easily switched to simple defensive mechanics. The soldier's focus became on not being caught off balance, parrying every one of Magicot's swings and keeping in step with every movement that he made. It took him a minute or so to recognize that there was some sort of deliberation in his opponent's defensive switch; it was as if he was buying time. Did the soldier know the mage was coming?

Magicot again found himself weakened and surprised by nothing less than the fear of the dragon fire-wielding mage. While worried that the soldier was stalling long enough for the mage to arrive, a dagger flew directly at Magicot and sunk deep into his left arm; and in that instant, the soldier took to the offensive, taking Magicot by surprise and forcing him off balance—and quickly, the fight was in the soldier's favor. If Magicot thought he could regain his edge, it disappeared quickly, especially since before Magicot could truly get into a defensive stance, another dagger came shooting at him from the woods, and he only just managed to avoid taking another hit from dagger or sword.

He tried to gain a balanced stance, but the soldier was very good at keeping his momentum and thus keeping his hold on the fight. The sword came in at his head almost with equal timing to a flying dagger aimed at his midsection, and although he could parry the sword with his spear, he just managed to miss dodging the dagger, receiving another cut in his side as the dagger passed by him.

A rustle in the trees awakened that survival instinct deep inside the god of chaos, and with a smile, he released a magical burst of energy that should have forced the soldier off his feet and flung him far away into the forest, giving Magicot the chance to run for it. Rocks were lifted off the ground and flung high into the air, bushes were uprooted, and even a small tree found itself moved far from where it had originally stood, but the soldier didn't budge despite seeming to be rather surprised by the sudden burst of energy and chaos around him.

Magicot was able to turn the stunned look in the soldier's face against him, managing to get a balanced foothold on the ground and giving himself a decent chance to defend himself from the soldier's relentless strikes. The most helpful thing that occurred though was that the daggers had stopped flying in at him, and Magicot expected his magical burst of energy had removed the invisible opponent from combat for at least a moment. Magicot did not enjoy this knowledge though for he could not understand how the young soldier continued to battle with such force and such precision. He should be lying down, shaken by the magical burst of energy, and Magicot should be running full sprint back to the rest of the Xile Tribe. Instead, Magicot was still doing everything he could to parry and dodge calculated swings of that sharp sword; and every time he saw an opportunity to turn to the offensive, the soldier would charge forward with his shoulder or place a well-timed kick on Magicot's lower shin, forcing him back into a defensive stance to parry the next incoming swing of that sharp sword.

Magicot had over a hundred years of practicing combat with the strongest fighters on the entire planet, but he had never had practice fighting against someone with such perfect precision, and Magicot was beginning to doubt his ability to win the fight and perhaps even his ability to flee. Magic had failed him already, and he could not understand why. Was another god in the forest protecting the young soldier from his magical powers? Perhaps a very powerful mage was in the trees, ready to counteract his every use of magical power. These thoughts were fleeting for though Magicot was ducking below another perfectly placed swing and then parrying the downward strike with the side of his spear, he asked himself why either would not simply join the fight. Confusion and lack of knowledge was distracting Magicot, and he was in dire need to find focus.

So as Magicot tried to use the length of his spear to create a small distance between himself and the soldier, he avoided relying on and using more magic because he did not know what kind of effect it might have, seeing as the first use of it had not quite gone as planned. He poorly blocked another swing from the incoming sword and received another gash in his side. The additional pain reminded him of the other cuts he had already taken, turning his mind to focus on the pain and the feel of the blood that was slowly traveling on his skin. Another swing and another poorly chosen block almost created an opening in Magicot's lower leg, and he was slowly losing the fight, trying his best to find some means to turn it in his favor, to find some means to survive.

Survival seemed to not be an option for Magicot for another dagger came zooming in his direction from behind a tree, and Magicot could not expect to be able to dodge it, and he was forced to use his magic yet again.

Relief flushed over him as the magical barrier he summoned blocked the incoming dagger, and then that relief vanished just as quickly as the sword passed through the barrier as though it wasn't even there. Magicot only just barely managed to guard against the swing with the back end of his spear, and then he jabbed the sharp end at the soldier in an attempt to back him up, but the soldier's precision carried to his movements as he so fluidly sidestepped the jab and swung his sword, forcing the spear away from him and almost unbalancing Magicot.

Another dagger zoomed in at Magicot then, and he only just barely got another magical barrier up to block it from colliding with the side of his head. He immediately found himself again parrying another swing of a sword that managed to pass through the barrier— not just as if it wasn't there, but because it was no longer there.

Magicot suddenly had a thought, and as he backed away from the swing, extending his spear forward to create a distance between himself and the soldier, he used his magic to summon a light in the dark and dreary forest. It shined all around, blinding both himself and his opponent temporarily; but once Magicot could see again, he was only disappointed to see the light reflecting normally off the long blade of the sword. He had been so sure that the sword had been what was absorbing his magic, but it was just a normal sword.

Although he hadn't found the source of his troubles, he did come to the conclusion that it was the soldier that was doing something to his magic since the barriers had indeed been able to block the thrown daggers. Perhaps magic could be used, just not directly on the soldier, and Magicot knew what to do. As the soldier came forward with a perfectly timed swing of the sword, Magicot began to back up, but as the soldier changed his motion to come forward and close the gap between them, he realized too late that Magicot had never actually stepped back, but had used an illusion. The magic, of course, vanished as the soldier got close enough to the illusion, but it was too late. The head of his spear had already found the stomach of the soldier, and magic-absorbing or not, Magicot had won the fight.

Hugheny stood completely still as he watched as Jahkan fall to his knees, clutching the hole in his stomach. He didn't know what it was he was feeling—anger? Hugheny didn't have friends because it was impossible to trust anyone when you worked in the black market, but if Hugheny could consider anyone a friend, Jahkan might have been the closest thing to one. The relationship between the two of them had simply been mutually beneficial; Hugheny received protection for his black-market deals in Duerken, and Jahkan had an easy way to receive difficult-to-procure items for an extremely cheap price. However, over the years, had that relationship felt different? Hugheny wanted to kill the barbarian who had just killed the skilled captain. He reached for more daggers to throw, but he couldn't find a single one.He had thrown them all.

The barbarian hadn't moved yet;he was standing there staring at Jahkan as he drew his last breath. Hugheny didn't care that it was at the risk of his own life;he charged toward the scene and was a little taken aback to see the magical barbarian running headlong in the opposite direction. He had lucked out, and Hugheny was sure the barbarian had probably thought him to be someone else, probably whomever he was running away from to begin with.

By the time Hugheny had reached Jahkan, it was too late for him to do anything, to even say good-bye. Jahkan was dead. He ignored the gaping hole in his stomach, and only the intent of killing the barbarian was flooding into his every thought. Perhaps it was because of that very overindulging thought that a few jewels in Jahkan's back pocket reflected the magical light into Hugheny's eyes, and he somehow knew exactly how to kill the magical barbarian.

———◆◆◆◆——

Magicot hadn't realized how long his duel with the soldier had truly lasted and was running for his life again, knowing that even with his illusion, that dragon fire-wielding mage was possibly just behind him again. It was helpful that a small amount of sunlight had begun to shine through the trees, but Magicot was moving at a slower pace than he had been earlier. The wounds he had received during his most recent fight were deeper than he originally noticed, and he had been losing quite a bit of his blood. He felt weaker with every step, and he didn't know how long he could possibly run before he would have no option but to stop.

Luckily for Magicot, a second wind kicked in; a survival instinct brought him back some strength as the sound of footsteps running in his direction traveled to his ears. He knew he was indeed being chased once more, and even if it wasn't the mage, but the knife thrower, Magicot didn't think he had enough in him for another fight. He could still use magic, but even that thought was not of great comfort as that had not been heavily reliable in his most recent fight.

Magicot couldn't keep going at the pace he wanted to, and a part of him knew he may need to stop and simply face his pursuer and hope beyond hope that it was not a deadly opponent. His mere want to survive pushed him forward, kept him going. It didn't matter that he was not able to put any distance between him and whoever was chasing him. It didn't matter even that the distance was getting smaller the longer he ran. They were getting closer, and although they never revealed themselves to Magicot, he knew who his pursuer was because Magicot heard the sound of a dagger cutting through the air in his direction.

Magicot turned and a magical barrier appeared to block the incoming dagger and Magicot felt safe. That feeling didn't last because he saw the dagger in the sunlight that had begun to peek through the trees, and unlike the sword, the dagger that was flying toward him only reflected the light off its jeweled handle. The blade absorbed the light. Magicot knew that dagger had belonged to the soldier he had killed, knew it beyond any doubt because the blade was made of *shadesteel,*a metal that not only absorbed light but absorbed magic.By the time Magicot recognized this to be true, to be fact, it was too late for him to react. The dagger had already passed through his barrier as if it didn't exist, and Magicot did not have time to dodge such a well-aimed throw. The only thought he could muster before the jeweled dagger dug its way deep into his brain was the thought of how long fifteen years would be.

WIND AND SWORDS

Hugheny was just barely keeping his eyes open as he sat just inside the cover of the trees at the edge of the forest. It was clear from their vantage point in the forest that the many members of the Xile that had spent their night in the town of Duerken were not expecting the battle to come to them. From what Hugheny could see from where he was, most of the Xile were cooking and eating, laughing and having a merry old time. Yes, this was not overly comforting to Hugheny as he had come to the conclusion already that they were a battle-hardened race, and despite their currently relaxed state, he knew all too well that they were far more ready for battle than they appeared.

The boats out on the ocean seemed to be moving again as they began to anchor in the water and move more warriors to shore. Hugheny knew that the lord of Duerken had been right in determining that now was the best time to attack. They weren't expecting it, and they were not quite as strong in numbers now as they would become if given another day.

Luckily for the town of Duerken, the numbers were once again on their side. It had been hours since Hugheny had killed the god of chaos, although at the time, he had not known that was who he was fighting. Dracut had seemed both disappointed and happy when Hugheny had told him the story, but Hugheny had been devastated to learn he had not made it back in time to save Vixxen. It was a small measure of comfort knowing he himself had avenged her death since he still felt guilty. Dracut, her husband, had constantly told him that morning that he wasn't to blame. His wife was a powerful mage, and with John and Jine, she was very well set to battle against a few barbarians. No one had known that they would be fighting a god. Dracut did, however, ask Hugheny to remember her death and put her memory to good use, to respect it.

So here he was, on the front line, re-equipped with many daggers, one bedecked with jewels, and the well-crafted sword that had once belonged to Jahkan Yute. He was prepared to fight in the name of a woman he hardly knew because he believed her life had been more valuable than his. It was a strange feeling for Hugheny to feel guilty, to feel responsible for any of his actions, but perhaps it was the threat that had come to Frendilar that made him feel more willing to fight, to protect his home. He didn't know what it was that had brought about this change in him, but he wasn't overly confident it was a healthy feeling.

He looked around him and was comforted by the many soldiers hidden among the trees. Both the towns of Huytle to the north and Restag to the west had sent their entire armies to the aid of Duerken. And above him in the tallest trees perched hundreds of deadly Woodnip archers, who had arrived that morning led by Dracut's best friend, Jaxxal. They were in the best possible position to make the Xile pay for the lives they took the prior day, and Hugheny was actually excited to be a part of it. Fear had no place in his mind. He was more ready for a fight than he had ever been in his entire life.

———◆◆◆◆◆———

Deerskyn should be in a great mood. After all, this was his war, or so others believed, but Deerskyn had known all along it had been Magicot who had manipulated him into starting this war, and it had already cost Deerskyn too much. But despite the losses, his men and women had taken over a town in just a day and were already unloading more warriors from their boats. Soon he would be joined by his best friend and most trusted general, and they would be able to charge forward and win the next battle.

Deerskyn wanted to feel triumphant and victorious, but it just didn't seem possible. He had lost his son in combat on only the first day to a most powerful enemy and had learned that there were more just like him. He had sent his shaman, the only member of the Xile that understood magic, to kill one of them, and he had never returned. Something, perhaps everything, about it was eating away at his insides, and his sister's constant warnings that Magicot had had no interest in winning a war, just in starting one, kept ringing in his head over and over again.

"Guards!" Deerskyn shouted. It was a strange reaction as both guards came running in the door to find their leader just standing in the middle of the room, safe and sound. Deerskyn's voice changed drastically in pitch as he went from sounding in trouble to giving off orders, and it was clear he was trying to catch his men off their guard. "How are we doing?"

The smaller of the guards was the quickest to respond, and Deerskyn knew he was like his own sister, always needing to get an extra footing because his size was against him. "We are just beginning to get boats 33 and 34 ready for emptying, sir."

"Good. Will we be able to reach fifty emptied boats by nightfall?"

"We should be able to," said the larger of the guards. "Is there a reason we are waiting to look for the next fight?"

Deerskyn looked at the larger warrior and recognized quickly the challenge that was hidden within those words. "I want the numbers. We still don't know our enemy."

"The enemy is running," said the larger guard as if this was the most important knowledge to the entire war. "Is it not our custom to cut down those who flee in fear?"

Deerskyn did not say anything because if he had known a giant magical tree was about to sprout from the ground and kill everything and anything within its reach, he felt he too would have run for it. Swords and brute strength would be of little use against such a large enemy. This was not a thought one could share among the Xile as it would immediately have been viewed as fear.

"They don't know or understand our customs," Deerskyn said. "But in case they did,them running away could have been a trap to bring us in. Or do you forget what happened to those who wanted to chase them?" Deerskyn saw a look of fear on both guards' faces as he brought up the magical tree. Both his guards had been lucky enough to survive the magical tree, but it was helpful to Deerskyn to know they had both been afraid of it just as much as he had been. "We are not fighting by our rules here in this land. We will pursue them when we have the numbers."

Both guards nodded as if this settled that, and Deerskyn began to decide where in this large town he should go to pass the day by. He wouldn't get a chance to decide as the sounds outside of the town changed in an instant. Singing and laughing stopped, music vanished, and screams and yells of battle and anger erupted. Deerskyn knew they were under attack, and that bothered him. If his enemy had chosen the offensive, then he knew they were not prepared to fight whatever it was that gave them the confidence to come.

❦

Jaxxal lifted his magical bow of air beside his Woodnip friends in the top of the trees, and as they released their living arrows, he let fly one of his magical arrows of air. The arrows passed over the Duerken's front wall, and the living arrows either found Xile flesh or came alive to seek out a foe. Jaxxal's arrow exploded on contact and released a major force of wind, picking up and blowing many Xile warriors every which way.

As they aimed again and released more arrows, the many Frendilar soldiers from nearby towns began to charge out of the forest and toward the town. A stampede of soldiers on horseback came riding out of the forest's path directed at the gate of the town that, luckily for the soldiers of Frendilar, the Xile did not know how to close. At the sight of Dracut charging out of the forest along with the soldiers, Jaxxal jumped out of the tree and rode a magical gust of wind to the ground beside his best friend. He had the speed to easily outpace him, to beat him to the town wall, but he chose instead to match his best friend's pace.

"Good luck, friend," Dracut said with such sorrow behind his voice Jaxxal became instantly worried that his friend did not want to survive the attack, but he knew there was nothing he could do or say. Dracut had lost the most important person in his life. He wanted to bring up Dracut's young daughter and how important he would one day be in her life. But he couldn't decide if such a tactic would weaken or strengthen a man in such despair.

"Make 'em pay" was all that Jaxxal said before turning off away from Dracut. Using his magical burst of speed, he ran directly up the wall that surrounded the town of Duerken, lifting himself to the top of it so fast, knowing he did not have a lot of time as he jumped off it and again caught a magical gust of wind that blew him deep into the middle of the town. He turned around just in time to watch the giant explosion of magical purple flames that tore down the wall he had just recently jumped off from, and a smile came to his lips as a rain of living arrows preceded the soldiers' charge into the town. Dracut was leading the charge, and the power of his deadly fiery maces did not waste any time finding an enemy.

Jaxxal was trying his hardest not to enjoy the fight, but he had been training all of his career for war in a land that had only known peace his entire life. This was his chance to put all his practice into true action, and as the first group of Xile warriors recognized his existence among them, he could do nothing but smile as they charged forward.

Five on one, and it was never even a contest. The nearly invisible magical blades of air that he summoned from his runic rods were more deadly than two swords of the same length because his opponents did not know what it was he was stabbing them with. And as he sidestepped two swings, he managed to put four holes into the chest of a large and deadly female warrior before any of her other tribe members had even managed to follow his movements.

Jaxxal was truly the deadliest of the mages, and this became apparent to all as he ripped apart Xile warrior after Xile warrior alone, outnumbered, in the middle of their ranks. Perhaps it was the chaos the attack had brought that made it so easy for him, but it was mostly just his speed. Years ago, he had come across the magic that gave him such speed, and it wasn't only his blades that could appear invisible. Jaxxal could move fast enough that many would find it near impossible to follow his movements; not being able to see your enemy was usually a problem and, in this case, consistently led to death.

Jaxxal spun around the swing of a long spear, ducked below a swinging sword, and put both his swords through the shoulders of a large Xile warrior; and before a single enemy could see him pull the swords of wind out of his most recent victim, he fell to the ground to roll under two more spears. He stood back up in a flash, and his swing removed the head of another Xile warrior; and as he moved for the center of town, his objective came into view.

He had listened to the account from Hugheny multiple times, but the description the young man had given did not do the towering leader of the Xile justice. He truly was a beast of a man, and even Jaxxal felt his goal to remove the leader may have perhaps been a miscalculation on his part. The enemy had underestimated magic, and suddenly, Jaxxal felt that he may have overestimated because the swords his opponent carried were nearly the size of Jaxxal himself.

With a deep breath, Jaxxal summoned a magical wind and was carried the remaining distance between himself and his enemy. Jaxxal's confidence rose as he recognized the fear on his enemies face.

Jaxxal landed only feet from Deerskyn, but he had misjudged how quickly the powerful leader could swing his giant-sized swords. Any other mage or soldier would have been dead from the misjudgment, but Jaxxal's speed saved him as he managed to react fast enough to get both his swords up to parry; the brute strength that was behind the swing had certainly required the two-sword parry, and this left him open for the quick and powerful swing of Deerskyn's second giant sword.

Jaxxal just managed to use magic to back out of his opponent's reach, and he knew that he now had to completely recalculate his opponent's speed and power. Two Xile warriors that had been behind their leader charged around him in the direction of Jaxxal, giving him no time to think about how to go about fighting their powerful leader who was Deerskyn. These new warriors were no different than the many Xile he had already killed since entering the battle for his hometown of Duerken.

"Stop!" Deerskyn yelled to his two warriors, but they either ignored him or just didn't have the time to listen; before either warrior even managed to come within reach of him, Jaxxal dashed forward, and neither Xile warrior had ever seen anyone move so fast. Both of them lay dead, cut in halves by the deadly swords of wind that Jaxxal fought with, and a smile spread across the mage's face as he recognized the anger and hatred on the face of Deerskyn.

Jaxxal knew how to use such anger in a fight, and he quickly charged Deerskyn again. As both giant swords came swinging in at the quick mage, he managed to avoid getting hit by one by stepping back quickly and then dashing back in, one sword up to parry the other sword, and the other angled downward just enough to nick the leader's shin. It drew blood and caused pain but was such a small cut it could not have done anything to a man of such pure muscle, but Jaxxal knew better. It would seem like nothing to an onlooker watching the fight, but Jaxxal knew that by making contact with his enemy's skin, he was adding fuel to the fire; and he knew he was right as Deerskyn reacted with anger, swinging both giant swords at him again.

Jaxxal quickly backed out of reach of the large swords again and immediately charged back in, managing to get two more small cuts onto the side of the deadly barbarian leader. Jaxxal was making Deerskyn angrier with each strike of his deadly swords, but Deerskyn was also learning to see and judge the length of those near-invisible swords, which became apparent with Jaxxal's next attack since he managed to just be out of reach to make contact.

Jaxxal had to quickly change tactics as his opponent managed to suddenly gain control of his anger. The large brute-strength swings became more calculated, and Jaxxal was just barely able to back out of reach of the first swing; but Deerskyn took a large step forward, closing the space before jabbing toward Jaxxal. Again, his magical speed was unmatched, and he quickly got himself far away from the incoming sword and was charging in again.

Deerskyn again showed how knowledgeable he had become in such a short time by using his immensely large swords to keep the speedy and agile mage just out of reach of making contact with his hard-to-see swords of wind. Jaxxal could see his opponent was learning quickly how to use his strength and power to keep Jaxxal back enough that he was unable to land an attack, and he soon found himself doing a lot more dodging and backing out than charging in.

Jaxxal managed to get a close swing into the left arm of his opponent, but Deerskyn ignored the pain completely, and his next swing lifted the small mage off his feet and knocked him feet away. Jaxxal was lucky that the collision of the swing had been with the barbarian's arm and not the blade of his sword because he was still quite alive, but the pain was real. As he stood up, he knew just how heavy a swing his opponent truly had, and Jaxxal had no desire to feel such contact again.

The barbarian leader saw a chance then, and he was the one charging headlong at the small mage. Jaxxal once again used his speed to just manage to get out of range of the large swinging swords, and he quickly dashed in as he had done so many times already. Both his swords were aimed at Deerskyn's heart, but Deerskyn backed up, keeping himself out of reach of those swords of wind.

Deerskyn's eyes stared into Jaxxal's with nothing but shock and confusion as the magically extended swords dug deep into the leader's heart. Deerskyn had judged the length of the magical blades but had ignored the simple idea that the length of the blades could change with magic, and Jaxxal had counted on that misjudgment. The mighty leader of the Xile Tribe fell dead to the ground, dead in combat because he failed to heed the warnings of his shaman,dead because he underestimated what magic could do.

Jaxxal turned toward the shore and the boats as the giant of a man, the leader of the Xile Tribe, lay on the ground. Deerskyn died instantly with a permanent look of confusion on his face, and Jaxxal, despite having defeated an opponent he had actually begun to think he couldn't beat, just walked away from the dead leader without ever looking back.

23

TAKING BACK THE SEA

The battle raged on, and Dracut, who was deep into the front lines, battled with no mercy for the murderous race. With each and every single swing of his magical maces, another Xile lost their life. The Xile Tribe could not possibly have prepared themselves for the pure massacre that came charging into what had so recently been their camp. The living arrows continued to be let loose from the back lines as the Woodnips joined in the close-range battles as well. The soldiers of Frendilar fought together as a team, and the chaos the Xile fought with and the complete lack of teamwork put them on two entirely different levels.

Frendilar and Woodnips alike were indeed losing lives in the fight, and there wasn't any true way to prevent that, but their teamwork and the absolute monster that was Dracut cutting a way into the town was greatly putting a gap between the number of Frendilar soldiers dead and the number of Xile warriors who were no longer breathing.

Dracut had not thought about his friend once as he continued to push forward, killing every Xile warrior that he could reach. Thoughts of his wife fueled his anger and hatred and thus fueled his relentless attacks that were leaving a trail of burning and melting flesh behind him. But when the Xile all began to run away, back toward the shore and their ships, Dracut's mind finally moved to his best friend, Jaxxal, who had taken it upon himself to remove the Xile leader from the picture. The sudden retreat of the Xile told Dracut that Jaxxal must have succeeded. A lot of the Frendilar soldiers were cheering at the sight of the retreating Xile, but Dracut urged them to pursue. Jaxxal would pursue; it had been his true father that had told them as teenagers that when you're bullied, you don't just fight back. You make sure they have a very good reason to never bully you again.

Hugheny quickly sided with Dracut's decision to pursue as did many of the Frendilar soldiers. They all knew it was important to strike fear into the hearts and even the souls of these merciless, barbaric killers because they might be leaderless and godless at the moment, but in time, they would get both back; andwhen they did, it was important that they knew it would be a bad idea to try and invade Frendilar again.

Hugheny followed the deadly mage in pursuit.The Xile were strong, but they were not fast, and the soldiers of Frendilar were quickly able to catch up to them. Hugheny recognized that their numbers seemed a bit smaller, and he looked behind to see that the Woodnips had chosen not to pursue, but they were not attempting to stop the humans from doing just that. The Woodnips recognized a win and would not create more death. Hugheny knew they had played their part, and it was up to the humans to make sure the enemy never returned. Soon Hugheny found himself dodging an incoming spear. He swung Jahkan's sword sideways, actually catching the blade directly on a weak part of the wood shaft and breaking the metal tip off the Xile's spear.

The Xile attempted to use his strength to his advantage as he charged directly at Hugheny, planning to crush the young thief with his giant muscles, but Hugheny quickly tossed a dagger into the heart of the charging Xile and then took the brunt of the charge as he put Jahkan's deadly sword in one side of the Xile's throat. He did not feel even remotely sick as he saw the blade jut out the other side covered in a new victim's blood.

Hugheny barely felt the hit of the giant barbarian's charge as the adrenaline he was feeling pumped him up and pushed him forward. Dracut began yelling for them to split up so they could pursue through the many different streets of the town, and without even thinking about why,Hugheny began heading north to the northern wall.

The direction Hugheny took was already mostly empty with just a few skirmishes going on between Frendilar soldiers who had encountered Xile warriors that had refused to flee and preferred to die along with their leader. The number of Xile willing to die for a man that was already dead was very few though it seemed, and he did not quickly find a fight he could join in until he passed a small alley where a small but skilled female Xile warrior was fending off three Frendilar soldiers.

"Hey," Hugheny shouted at the soldiers, "back away from her!" The soldiers turned in shock at first, but they did indeed listen and back away from the woman Xile. They were looking at the small man the lord of Duerken had put in charge of the soldiers that were on foot, and he knew they were looking for a reason why he had told them to back off; he wasn't entirely sure why he had done so himself.

Hugheny was only happy the woman was taking the reprieve as a chance to breathe and not a chance to retaliate; and as Hugheny came closer to the female Xile himself, he finally spoke again. "Pursue with the others. This is the enemy that tied me up.She's mine."

"Are you sure you don't want us to stay and help?She is pretty deadly."

"Go!" Hugheny shouted. "I and I alone will kill this one." The anger in his voice was clear and direct, and quickly, the soldiers nodded and ran out of the alley, looking to pursue and find another enemy to fight.

Hugheny turned to the woman who had hit him over the head and tied him and subjected him to the terrors of Deerskyn. He looked at her with a reminder that it had been the fact that she had captured him that had eventually led to the death of Vixxen. He raised the sword of Jahkan, recognizing that his death had come at the hands of the god that had been sent out after Vixxen as well. "This is what they call payback in Frendilar."

Jaxxal reached the docks quickly, and with a very fast running start and the help of his magical wind, he soared off the dock and landed gracefully on the deck of a boat anchored far out at sea. Most of the boats that still had Xile aboard them had recognized the call of retreat and had already turned around and begun to sail away. Jaxxal was happy to find that his magical sword of wind was quickly able to cut through the anchor's chain, and he raised his hands up over his head, and the wind swords connected to stretch out into a long staff of wind. This allowed Jaxxal to put a lot of focus into his magical abilities, and soon the wind was circling around the boat he was on alone, lifting it into the air, and within just a few minutes, he had turned the large ship around and dropped it back into the ocean. The wind began to blow into the sails, pushing his ship forward in pursuit of those that were fleeing.

At first, he didn't think he would be able to catch one of the fleeing boats, but suddenly, the ship he was steering using nothing but magical bursts of wind was lifted into the air by a huge wave that was unnaturally traveling away from the shore. The wave helped him close the distance he needed to catch up to the closest fleeing ship.

At first, Jaxxal could not figure out what had happened, what kind of luck he had just run into. Then he noticed the water close to the beach had turned a rather deep shade of red. The Xile warriors that were charging into the water in an attempt to swim to the anchored boats were finding themselves being cut to pieces by hundreds of Seachurns that were waiting in the water for them. Jaxxal smiled as he looked around for his wife, and although he knew she had been the one that gave him the boost with the ocean wave, he could not find her. He expected that perhaps she was in the water or possibly she was among the many Seachurns now boarding some of the anchored boats that were trying to turn around.

———◆◆◆◆◆◆———

Juhni's long staff of water seemed to confuse the Xile warriors on the boat. They had obviously never seen a magical weapon before, but her first two victims very quickly learned how deadly that staff could be when hit over the head by it for the water acted like solid metal, and the first Xile warrior she hit was quickly unconscious on the deck of the ship. A female warrior charged after her next, but she quickly learned how deadly that weapon of water was as it changed shape into a trident, and a quick jab created three deep holes in the woman's chest and stomach.

Juhni was not alone on the ship either; over a dozen Seachurn warriors had boarded the boat with her, including the Seachurn princess Asrien. Asrien was a better fighter in a group than she was alone, and Juhni had never seen such a paired precision of attacks as those of Asrien and her fighting partner, Jewly. They fought as if they were dancing back to back, side to side; it didn't seem to matter. Every Xile warrior that attempted to fight the pair was moving into a two-on-one, and although the Seachurn women seemed small compared to the barbarians, their agility and precision in battle made them the deadly ones.

Asrien ducked below a high-swinging sword and circled around the back of her opponent. Her pair, Jewly, came forward with her single sword jabbing at the Xile's stomach. When he backed away from the incoming sword, he was not in a position to block or dodge the quick punches of Asrien. Her golden knuckles hit him in the head three times, and he dropped to the ship's deck with a broken skull. Asrien quickly fell back into step with her fighting partner, and Juhni wished she could just watch the pair fight for hours for they were so in sync. But she did not have the luxury because although the agile movements of the Seachurns were quickly defeating the many Xile warriors on the boat, Juhni wanted to finish them off quicker for she had just helped get her husband a chance to catch the fleeing ships, and she wanted a chance herself to catch up with him.But every minute they were fighting on this anchored ship, the fleeing ships got farther away; and the speed at which her husband was able to move the ship he was on with his magical wind, she knew he'd be out of sight soon enough.

Her magical trident collided with an oncoming spear, and as she quickly turned it over and jabbed her trident forward, it connected with the arm of the Xile. He didn't even react, and Juhni recognized that her opponent didn't feel pain as he grabbed her watery trident and pulled it out of his own arm. He grasped it, holding onto it and used his pure strength to pull Juhni close to him. Juhni almost laughed as the trident turned to ice suddenly, and the part that the Xile warrior was holding broke off with a quick upward pull on her weapon. Before the warrior could react, he had a sharp, broken staff of ice through his head. The ice turned to water again that fell to the deck of the ship, creating a puddle.

Another warrior thought that was her chance to take on Juhni, but they truly did not understand magic at all because one minute Juhni was unarmed and then the next, she had another trident of water dug deep under the ribs of the charging warrior. It was only then that a group of four warriors decided to take her on at once. Juhni was outnumbered, but she had magic, and they did not. She ran from them, and this seemed to give them confidence as they charged after her, but as she jumped off the ship into the ocean, a wave came up to catch her. The part of the wave that was holding her up continued forward, and as it towered over the part of the ship that the four warriors were still on, the wave crashed down on them, immediately freezing them all into a single block of ice.

⬥━◈━⬥

Dracut soon reached the shore, and he realized then that there were no more enemies for him to hit with his fiery maces. The Seachurns had arrived, and the human soldiers and the Seachurn warriors had created a pincer, and none of the large barbarian warriors had survived. Dracut looked out at the ocean and could see that many ships were being won over by the Seachurn warriors, and the rest of the ships had now almost sailed out of sight. Dracut knew that Jaxxal was out there, chasing down a boat or two.

Jaxxal had grown up in Duerken, and before he turned fifteen and found out he was a mage, he used to sail the seas with the fishermen. True, Dracut had never seen a ship or boat anywhere near the size of these that the Xile had sailed across the ocean in, but he had faith that his friend could sail one alone with magic.

Without an enemy to kill, Dracut could finally look around and see the thousand or so dead bodies that littered the town. Their victory was small though for many had lost someone they loved today. Dracut thought about his wife and then looked up at the large weeping willow that towered over the ocean shore. Isaic had been a friend of his, not quite as close as Jaxxal or Juhni, but a friend nonetheless. They had lost two of their most powerful mages in this battle, and as John and Jine stopped beside him and looked up at the willow, they both lowered their heads in respect, and Dracut followed suit.

"A victory," said the lord of Duerken behind them. "A victory wellearned but not necessary. It almost feels like we lost so much and gained nothing from this. What is the point of any of this?"

"Chaos," whispered Dracut. John and Jine turned to him. "This war was brought by chaos. There was no point to it."

"Is there ever a point to war?" the lord asked.

"Our father would say peace is the point of war," John piped in.

"They weren't looking for peace," said Dracut, "and we already had it."

"Then as you said, it is," said the lord, "a pointless war. We lost many lives for absolutely nothing."

"No," said Dracut. "My wife didn't die for nothing. She died for the lives of those who didn't die." No one said anything in response. The truth of the matter was, although they had won and chased away the invading army in just a day, there would be little celebrating. His wife might have not died for nothing, but Dracut knew deep down she hadn't needed to die at all. This was nothing more than a god's twisted idea of fun, and Dracut couldn't help but wonder if all the gods were similar.

24

ANOTHER GOD

The deeper into the caves Shavore walked, the darker they became as the dragon's-breath torches became more spread out. He could hear the heavy breathing of the beast long before he entered the massive cave-like room—nearly as large as the room he had first introduced himself to Dracut in. He entered slowly into the cave, and as he entered, the heavy breathing stopped, and it quickly turned to a growl.

A little girl's hushed voice was heard in the darkness as it relaxed the large black dragon. Shavore lit a torch and placed it on the wall, and then he could see his sister's pet dragon. The dragon could barely fit itself in the room and had to stay lying down in order to avoid hitting its large scaly head on the rock ceiling. Shavore was glad they had brought the dragon down to this cave when it was just a baby. Now that it had grown full size, the dragon was trapped, unable to fit through the tunnels of the mountain.

Shavore could feel the hot breath of the dragon on his face, but the dragon's fire would not harm him, and the dragon knew it. The dragon feared Shavore as well; it wasn't afraid of its own pain or for its own life, but Shavore had learned the dragon's weakness years ago. As he got closer to the dragon, it backed away, giving view for the first time of a very young Ashen, his sister.

"Hello, brother," said the girl in a sweet and innocent voice. Shavore bent down and handed her two dead rats, and she looked at them hungrily. "Thank you." She quickly dug her fangs into the first dead rat, and Shavore could see her savoring the blood and flesh from the small animal. It wasn't a sign of evil like so many thought; it was merely the way of the Ashen.

While his sister ate the rats, he took the time to check her chains. They were securely wrapped around both her wrists and ankles, and he could clearly tell they were still just as connected to the cavern floor as they had been when he had first installed them. Even the large dragon did not have the power to break through the shadesteel bindings. Shavore was glad to see his sister was still chained up securely, and as she finished picking the meat of the bones of the second rat, he turned to her. Her dragon was still pressing itself up against the back wall because it knew that if it even appeared to be threatening Shavore, the girl would take his full retaliation.

"Grace," Shavore said, "how does it go?"

Grace closed her eyes, and her long black hair turned colors, first to gray and then yellow before reaching a fiery orange and actually turning to flames. Shavore just watched as his little sister used the powers she was born with—the powers Shavore had plans to take full advantage of. He had had years to plan the downfall of the mages, but it wasn't until his sister was born did he find the way to accomplish his goals.

His patience slowly drained away as he waited, watching his teenage sister's hair burn bright; and then when he felt he couldn't wait any longer, it went out, turning back to its young pitch-black color, and Grace opened her eyes.

"Well?" Shavore said impatiently.

"They've won," she said.

"As I knew they would," Shavore said. "I will admit they managed a lot quicker than I ever thought they would. The mages are powerful, but they don't know how powerful they are."

"And you want that power."

188

Shavore smiled. His sister had a knack for understanding him so well.

"I want my power," he said with annoyance, "the power that is rightfully mine, that she took from me. I retained powers, but it's limited in this physical form."

"Well, your plan worked," his sister said with a bit of a frown. "Perhaps not quite as you expected it to. Your counterpart ran from Dracut, but he still died."

"I had expected Dracut to kill Magicot, but it doesn't matter. The plan is not affected by who killed him, but merely by the fact that one god is out of the picture for the next fifteen or so years."

"Do you not think he would have wished to help you?"

"Magicot assist me?" Shavore had to laugh. "It is true, I'm sure he misses the ability to cause chaos with his old unrestricted powers, but his focus is entirely on chaos. My plan requires precision and patience."

His little sister shrugged then, and anger flushed his face. Was she keeping something from him? He didn't know what she could be keeping from him. She had told him that Frendilar had won just like he knew they would. Magicot, god of chaos, had not survived the battle either, and that was good news as far as Shavore was concerned.

"Anything else you would like to tell me?"

His sister smiled, and he knew she was indeed keeping what was obviously a juicy secret from him. "The mage's best friend, the one you hoped to take advantage of with your plan, is in deep pursuit of the Xile."

"What do you mean *deep pursuit?*"

Grace smiled. "At sea. He's chasing them on a ship, and he does not seem to have any intent of slowing down his pursuit."

"Does this affect my plan in some way?" Shavore began to rack his brain as to why this small bit of news was so important.

"A storm is brewing," Grace said, still smiling up at her brother in a victorious sort of way. "He will likely not find his way home in short time."

Shavore had practiced patience for many years, but now that he finally had a chance, had finally found the perfect distraction that he could use to start moving forward, he did not have the patience to wait again.

"If he doesn't, I'll find another way."

The smile vanished from Grace's face. "His wife died." There it was; the true secret she was hiding from him.

"That I can use," Shavore said with a grin. He tossed his sister a dead rabbit, her preferred meat, and he knew that this treat of sorts was the only reason she had given him the information. She was looking to hold it from him so she could get more, hoping the first bit of news would be enough for the treat, but Shavore had seen through the ruse and had held it till she told him exactly what it was he needed to hear.

"My lord." Shavore turned to see his mother in the cavern entrance. He was done here anyway. He walked away from his sister and her dragon, taking the torch with him and leaving the two in pitch blackness in their large prison.

"Any news?" Profilli asked.

"Everything is going according to plan," said Shavore as he placed the torch back on the wall of the cavern, and they entered the small room with the table. Lying on the table, tied to it with rope, was a small humanoid being. Not human, but a Woodnip. A little disappointment crossed Shavore's facial expression when he noticed it was a Woodnip child. The Woodnips were small and bony, and it was difficult to truly get flesh and blood out of a full-grown Woodnip—but a child, he might as well be eating scraps.

"This is all that ventured into the ruins?" Pro nodded, and Shavore sighed in disappointment. "When you told me that someone had ventured into the ruins, I was hoping it meant finally having a real meal for once."

"I left him alive for you at least," Pro said. "I know how you like to play with your food."

Shavore walked over to the table and looked down on the helpless and scared Woodnip child. He was shaking in fear, and Shavore did smile at his mother then. She did know him so well.

"Well?"

Shavore just looked at her. "Soon," he said. "Soon I will be able to begin my plans. I will wipe the mages' entire existence out entirely. And then, and only then, will I be safe to seek out the way to end this curse. Only then will I be able to seek out the way to get my true powers back."

Shavore looked down on the pitiful Woodnip child and continued his speech to the boy. "They took them from me. And every day these mages use magic that was once mine to bring peace and love, happiness, even, to the world. Hatred has been so lacking in the last hundred years, but I have a plan, a plan to bring all that hatred back."

The small boy gave off a squeak of fear, which turned into a scream of pain as Shavore grabbed and twisted the Woodnip's leg until he heard it break. The screams echoed through the caves, and Shavore just smiled.

"Do you know who I am?" he asked. The Woodnip just continued to scream in pain, and great pools of tears began to stream down the face of the child. "I asked do you know who I am?" And with a great force and the claws of an Ashen, Shavore tore the Woodnip's leg off at the knee, and the boy screamed again, never answering his evil torturer.

"I am Haidier, the one and only god of hatred," he said to the world. "And when every mage is dead and hatred once again is spread throughout the entire kingdom of Frendilar, I will regain my powers, and I will make the entire world pay for my curse, for my suffering." His voice echoed in the chamber next to him. As he sunk his teeth into the Woodnip's leg and as he savored the dripping blood and the juicy flesh, he was reminded of the weaknesses he held being trapped in an Ashen's body. Weaknesses like the need to eat, the need to survive. When he was a god, he was all powerful, and he would be a god again.

But first, the mages had to be removed from the picture, for as long as they were alive, as long as they were watching over Frendilar, anything Shavore tried to do would get back to them.And if they discovered who he was and what he was capable of, he'd be stopped. He was reminded of the truth, the fact that the mages had the powers of the gods, and he was trapped in an Ashen's body, left with only a limited amount of his original powers.

"They think this war they've won is over," Shavore said over the tears and the sound of the crying Woodnip as he slowly bled out on the stone table, "but it hasn't even begun yet."

25

AFTERWARD

The sound of battle had disappeared from the shore of Duerken, and the only sounds that remained were those of exhaustion and cheers of victory. The Duerken soldiers and a few others were not in the mood to cheer the victory because for them, the victory had come at too high a price. Juhni was among those in a victorious mood as she put foot to land for the first time in almost a day. Two female Seachurns followed her onto the beach, Asrien and Asrien's appointed commander, Jewly. Jewly was just as gorgeous as the rest of the female Seachurns and held her own even beside the princess Asrien. With black hair and a very light complexion, she was a beauty that was more of a contrast to the beauty that was her superior, Asrien.

"Seems we arrived just in time," Asrien said behind Juhni, "although I wonder how important our arrival was."

"The pursuit of the retreating army is just as important as the initial battle," said Juhni. "We arrived in time to put a wrench in their planned retreat, and thus, if they were planning to back off and regroup, we gave them reason to second-guess that plan."

Jewly laughed as she looked out at the sea where, by this time, no moving ships were visible still on the dark horizon. "I believe your husband is continuing to see to that."

"Still no sign of him then?" Juhni was worried. Her husband had sailed the sea before as he had grown up here in Duerken as a child. But when he was younger, he did travel too far out and had been lost at sea; Juhni was not okay with the idea of her husband getting lost out there again. He'd been lucky, getting stranded on some island where he managed to survive till he was able to repair his ship and leave the island. Could he get such luck again?

"We sent a few scouts out to look, but the ships are all moving at too fast a pace for them to keep up," said Asrien. "They lost them about an hour or so ago and returned." Juhni just nodded. The sun was setting and the clouds had grown dark over the ocean's horizon, and she knew it might be a while before she would see Jaxxal again. She wanted to have faith, to be able to hope that he'd find his way back to her quickly, but she knew better. Jaxxal was the only one ever capable of making her feel hope or faith, and as long as he was away from her, it would be hard for her to be optimistic.

"You know, you two could have returned home with the rest of your army." Juhni looked at the only two Seachurns who had chosen to stay behind after victory had been won. She allowed herself to think past her husband, knowing all too well he could take care of himself.

"We aren't going back at all," said Asrien. Jewly turned to the princess then in a quick act of shock and surprise, but Juhni got the feeling the surprise was not due to the content of the statement but due to the fact that it was spoken aloud. Asrien looked to Jewly and confirmed Juhni's feelings. "I trust her."

Jewly looked at Juhni, and Juhni suddenly became very confused; she knew it must have shown on her face.

"We are in love," said Jewly.

"And you saw how that is treated in our home," Asrien said. "It was why I volunteered to lead the army myself. It was a chance to escape the island. I knew I wasn't going to be returning."

Juhni understood all too well, and her mind flashed back to watching the two Seachurn women's silent screams as they boiled to death. "Do you have a plan?" Both Seachurn women shook their heads, and Juhni allowed herself to smile. "Then perhaps you'd be willing to stick with me for the time being. I may know a good town in the western kingdom that would be very happy to take on a few Seachurn warriors for the royal guard."

Juhni's smile grew as both Seachurns smiled. "Thank you," said Asrien.

"It's the least I can do."

⬥◦✦◦⬥

Hugheny could feel the pain now that his adrenaline had settled back down. The pain of the large gash in his lower ankle, the pain of the bruise on his head, but most importantly, the pain of guilt that continued to remind him that Vixxen and Jahkan's deaths were, to at least some extent, his fault. He was bent low over another body, this one a Duerken soldier, and this one he knew. His name was Darrel Longenn, and he was a good man. The guilt didn't travel to the deaths beyond those that had occurred in the forest, but he still felt different than he thought he would if ever such a battle would occur.

His name carried across the darkening sky in a strong and commanding voice. Hugheny turned and found the lord of Duerken walking in his direction at that very time. He wondered when he would finally have to pay for all his past and current crimes. With the war going on, Frendilar had needed every soldier willing to fight, every spy willing to enter enemy territory; but now that it was over, the lord was sure to finally arrest one of the black-market traders he had been after for such a long time.

The lord of Duerken was followed closely by two soldiers that Hugheny recognized from the meetings earlier that morning. He stopped beside Hugheny and looked down at the body that Hugheny had been inspecting. "We've lost a lot of good men and women."

"Do we have a plan for cleanup?" asked one of the soldiers following the lord.

"I did hope that soldiers of Huytle and Restag would stick around to help with the cleanup and perhaps a bit of the rebuilding needed to help move the citizens of Duerken back into their homes."

"Of course," said the other soldier. "The soldiers of Huytle will stick around for however long it takes. This is an absolutely terrible situation."

"And we are all in it together," added the other soldier. "Restag will be of whatever use it can."

The lord of Duerken nodded to the soldiers and then turned to Hugheny. "Hugheny, I would like you to meet Gransen, captain of the guard for Huytle, and Travis, captain of the guard for Restag." Hugheny nodded to the two captains, expecting them to arrest him there on the spot.

"If he chooses to accept," the lord said, now directing his words to the soldiers as well as Hugheny, "Hugheny here is my newly appointed captain."

Shock and surprise were not strong enough words to describe the sudden feelings that Hugheny felt as what the lord had said sunk in. He was giving him a second chance to do right, a chance to respect the death of Jahkan Yute. "Of course I accept."

"Then I entrust the cleanup to the three of you. I must go and speak to the mages." Hugheny was still in shock as the lord of Duerken walked away in search of Dracut and Jaxxal. He turned to the other captains and only then realized he had just been given a chance—not only a second chance to do right, but also a second chance to live. Perhaps a family was possible now, at least in the near enough future. However, a difficult time was ahead of them.

"We will need to contact the mages," Gransen said. "They will surely be gathering resources from their many academies in the western kingdom for war. They should be informed that it has been resolved."

"Magic can do some pretty amazing things," Hugheny added. "Informing them we could use help in rebuilding and getting the citizens of Duerken back into their homes would also prove to be useful."

"Agreed," Huytle added. "I have just the right messenger." And just like that, the war was over; and as far as anyone could tell, peace would take control again.But for some, peace would never again be an option.

———————————————

Dracut was already hard at work while those around him celebrated their victory. He worked on moving the rubble from the wall he destroyed in preparation for magically putting the entire wall back together with the help of some very hot fire.

Night had nearly settled in by the time the lord of Duerken found Dracut. He didn't immediately inform Dracut of his presence, and so Dracut continued his work, placing a large rock on top of another, nearly completing half of the wall that he had broken in. The sweat from the entire day was continuing to build up under his white mage robes, but it wasn't until he stopped for a light breather did he even notice.

"You would think there would be a magical way to make that a bit easier," said the lord. Dracut turned to him but couldn't bring himself to smile.

"Hello, Lortael," Dracut said. Lortael laughed.

"I forgot what it is like to hear my name spoken aloud."

"Sorry, my lord." Despite the mock bow that Dracut added to the statement and the joking manner he brought out in Lortael's presence, Dracut had little to smile about.

"Much better," Lortael joked, laughing quite enough for the two of them. He grinned in an attempt to frown. "Sorry, I know you don't quite see this as a victory."

Dracut didn't say anything; Lortael did not need to apologize to him. He understood that for many, they had just won the first war or even battle they had fought in over a hundred years, and despite their losses, history stated and showed that prior wars held much greater losses. But Dracut had lost the war, had lost it in a personal way. When his daughter finally turned fifteen and joined him at the mages' tower, what would he tell her?

Dracut lifted another rock and tossed it onto the pile, slowly rebuilding the large wall that protected the town of Duerken. "It might be easier with magic, but it's the physical labor that keeps me from having to think about what it is I've lost."

A woman's voice was the first to respond to Dracut. "Lost?" Dracut turned around quickly to see Juhni walking toward him with two very pretty women walking behind her. Dracut suspected they were two of the Seachurns that Juhni had come to battle with.

"Vixxen," Lortael explained so that Dracut would not have to. "She was killed protecting the fleeing citizens late last night." Silence fell among the entire group, and Dracut went back to work on the wall.

"I'm sorry," Juhni said softly to him.

"So am I," added Dracut. He knew she understood him more than anyone would. Vixxen had been Juhni's friend before she had been Dracut's wife. Just as Jaxxal had been Dracut's friend before Juhni's husband. "Where's Jaxxal?" Dracut asked, suddenly looking around,sure his best friend should have come to his side and worked alongside him in silence as he had done when his true father had died so many years ago.

Juhni and both Seachurn women turned and looked off at the ocean, and Dracut stopped working, stopped using his physical muscles to work off his despair. If Jaxxal had not returned from the ocean by now, would he ever? Was he dead as well? Dracut had expected his best friend to be the one to comfort him through this tough time. Dracut had been counting on his best friend to keep him sane in the next few months as he mourned his wife's death. Dracut suddenly felt true fear, fear for his own mental stability.

EPILOGUE

As night fell, Hugheny found himself exhausted from the entirety of his day. Physical exhaustion had hit first, but as he stood inside of the old home of Jahkan Yute, he reached a level of mental and emotional exhaustion as well. Because of him, a good man had died, and he had been unable to save him; and instead of being punished, Hugheny almost felt as though he was being rewarded. He had just been appointed Duerken's Captain of the Guard, and with it came a home as well. Jahkan's old home.

"It's a nice place," Effauna said, coming in from the small cooking area in the back of the home. "Cozy, at least in comparison to the huts I've lived in all my life." Hugheny turned to the Xile woman he had saved but said nothing. Hugheny had decided it would be best to have her lie low for a while. He was fortunate that Effauna did not share her brother's stature for she not only fit nicely into the normal clothes of a Duerken woman, but in them, she easily passed as a human.

"Still thinking about the man who used to live here?" Hugheny nodded as he looked around the room again. "It's not your fault he died."

"I still have trouble seeing it that way."

"Yes, you told my brother where the Taille woman was, but if it wasn't for that information, he would have sent hundreds of men down that path, and a lot more civilians would have probably died.

He would have wanted to be prepared for the unknown, and thanks to you, he thought he was prepared enough."

Hugheny just shook his head. Had he saved lives, or was Effauna just trying to make him feel better? It was hard to know for sure because she was certainly intelligent enough to lie to him, and he did not understand the world she was from.

"You look human," Hugheny said to change the subject. She turned in a circle, looking down at the simple cloth dress he had found for her.

"I feel weird," she said as she came to a stop. "I'm so used to less but tighter coverings."

"You'll get used to it."

"I expect so." Effauna gave him a smile, and Hugheny found himself blushing slightly. "Do you really think I can pull it off?"

"The only concern I had was your muscular build, but you told me you often worked with the weapon makers in your village back home. I figure you can find some work as a blacksmith in town, help rebuild the town, maybe. It would be both useful and give you a cover that will be believable."

Hugheny felt comfortable around Effauna, and it was not easy to explain. She just stood there smiling at him, and he knew she was just as comfortable with him.

A knock at the door wiped that smile off her face, and Hugheny felt a small bit of disappointment in the scowl that took its place.

"Are you expecting someone?" she asked. Hugheny nodded and walked to the door. He put his hand on the knob and saw the hesitant step toward the kitchen that Effauna took. Hugheny shook his head; he knew he had to test her cover with others.

He opened the door and invited in two mages dressed in long white Taille mage robes.

"Looks like things have turned out all right for you," John said to Hugheny as he closed the door behind them.

"Nice place," Jine said next. Jine noticed Effauna then, and he elbowed his brother. The twins gave a small head bow to the woman.

"Sorry for the intrusion," John said. "Perhaps we can make this quick and get out of here."

Effauna made a fake but convincing smile. She slowly nodded her head as well to the two mages. "Please, take all the time you need." She then turned and went into the kitchen area to leave Hugheny with the two mages.

"Things really seem to have worked out for you," said Jine once the three men were alone.

"It's a bit uncomfortable, actually," Hugheny said truthfully.

"We understand completely." John looked at the white robes he and his brother were wearing. "We've always hoped we'd become Tailles, but the trouble with wishing that is a prior Taille has to step down or die. And they were all so young."

"We never thought we'd get here this young ourselves," Jine continued. "It's a bit bittersweet. Vixxen was a wonderful Taille, and it's only because of her death this was even possible." Silence fell between the three men then, and it wasn't until they heard the crashing of pots in the kitchen that the silence was broken.

"Sorry!" Effauna yelled, and Hugheny couldn't help himself and let out a small chuckle.

"Lovely," John said with a smile. "Anyways, we need to get some rest ourselves. What is it you wanted to talk to us about?"

"Right," said Hugheny. "You two going to stick around for a bit to help with the cleanup?"

"Of course," Jine said. "You can count on us."

"Will you be returning to the academy after?"

"Only to say good-bye." John's gaze turned to his robe again. "Then it's back to the tower. Why?"

Hugheny gave a deep sigh then pulled out the shadesteel dagger he had stolen for Jahkan and handed it to Jine. The jewels sparkled in the light from the nearby lantern, and Jine stared at it with confusion.

"It belongs to the academy," Hugheny said to clear things up. "I sort of stole it for a client, was hoping you could return it for me."

Jine looked at him, and a huge smile came across his face. "Looks like you really are turning over a new leaf." Hugheny smiled because he knew he truly was.

———— ❖ ————

The clouds covered the sky as far as Jaxxal could see, which wasn't very far. The rain was coming down so hard it made it impossible to see far in the night sky, and there wasn't a single visible star to help Jaxxal get his bearings. He had been certain a few hours before that he was traveling in the right direction to return home, but now that so much time had passed, he had begun second-guessing himself. He had fought with the ship and the current to try to get the right course, and he no longer had any idea which direction he needed to go.

Even with magic at his disposal, sailing the ship alone was proving to be very difficult, and the current storm was making it near impossible. The wet sails did not respond as gently to his magical gusts of air, and the natural wind continued to try and blow in the opposite direction that Jaxxal wanted it to blow, so his magical wind was in battle with the natural wind.

The waves of the ocean had grown unsettled as well as the night continued on, and Jaxxal was beginning to wonder if he'd be lost at sea again. It had happened to him before when he was just a boy. Long before he was old enough to use magic, he had gotten lost at sea with his first father and their crew. He had lost him when the boat ran ashore on an island during a storm just like this one, and Jaxxal had been the only survivor.

Lightning lit up the sky, but it didn't give Jaxxal any true visibility; it gave him view of nothing useful that he could use to navigate home, and as he attempted to gain control of the ship, he realized he was only losing it. The boat no longer turned when he wanted it to, and turned when he had finally decided he wanted it to stay put. Jaxxal began to wonder if nature was actually out to get him, or if he was trying so hard to get control it was actually him trying to do whatever the weather wouldn't let him.

As another bolt of lightning erupted from the dark clouds overhead, Jaxxal knew he needed to get below deck to protect himself. But as he tried to get across the deck, he realized he had been much better staying put during the storm because it was near impossible to hold himself upright and balanced as he crossed the deck of the swaying ship. He felt himself falling, and only because of his unnaturally fast reflexes did he manage to keep from going overboard.

Jaxxal held on to the side of the boat for dear life, waiting for the right moment to try to sprint across the deck so as to get below. Another bolt of lightning shot from right above him then, striking the mast of the ship; and although the rain helped put out the small flames quickly, the damage to the ship could not be repaired during the storm, and Jaxxal found himself worried he might not only end up lost at sea, but he was no longer confident he'd be able to survive the storm.

———◆◆◆◆◆———

Jaxxal didn't know how many days the dark storm continued on, but he was no longer strong or healthy. He'd barely managed to keep himself alive and had used every ounce of magical strength he could muster to keep the boat floating on the water. The lightning strikes had become more common over the last few hours, and he knew he was weak. The need to survive had taken over his need to sleep, but the need to survive had now become one and the same with the need to rest his body and his spirit.

Another strike of lightning lit up the sky, but it was far in the distance now. The rain had stopped, but it was of little use to Jaxxal for what had followed the rain was a blanket of fog so thick he could barely see his own hands when inches in front of his face.

There was little hope left in Jaxxal; no optimism remained, and whatever confidence he had had disappeared with his strength. He leaned up against the ship that was being held together with almost magic at this point; it had taken so much damage.And as his eyes began to close, that magic began to falter. He couldn't continue to hold the boat together while he slept, but he no longer had the strength to stay awake.

His eyes closed, and all around him, the ship fell to pieces. Splintered wood and burned sails were all that floated around him in the water as he began to sink into the ocean. He was falling asleep, and the thought of his wife was the only thing keeping him awake, trying to get him to wake up, to fight to survive, but he did not have the ability to survive.

It was lucky for Jaxxal that lots of tiny hands grabbed a hold of his limbs just then and lifted him out above the water. He felt as though he were flying, but he couldn't manage to open his eyes enough to look around and see what was going on, at least not until he felt himself fall a few feet face-first into a large pile of sand. He opened his eyes more from the pain in his face than the need to see who had saved him.

Surrounding him were six small but colorful people. They reminded Jaxxal of the Woodnips but were about half the size and had much less subtle skin colors, such as a bright purple and deep pink. They were all girls, all with long hair that hung into the sand below their feet. And their feet were not touching the ground for they were flapping their large insect-like wings, hovering just above the sand.

The bright orange-skinned Khixki put her feet to the ground, and her wings came to a stop on her back as she bent over looking very closely at Jaxxal. Jaxxal looked up into her face and her long silver hair. She was looking at his silver hair as well, and he saw her shake her head.

"You were not supposed to return, Jaxxal."

Jaxxal closed his eyes as the goddess of peace shook her head at him, and the other Khixkis she had created shook their heads as well. Jaxxal did not respond as he felt safe enough to finally fall asleep.

ABOUT THE AUTHOR

Timothy Rivard was born in Leominster, Massachusetts in 1986. Although he did not dream of being an author at a young age, he enjoyed having a unique and powerful imagination as a child. He graduated from Fitchburg State University in 2011 with a Bachelor of Arts degree in mathematics and a minor in professional writing with a focus in creative writing. Although by the time he reached college, he dreamed of being an author. He supported his wife and three kids by working in the fast food industry and later, as a customer service representative, but he never gave up on his dream of inviting readers into his mind and sharing his wild imagination.

CPSIA information can be obtained at www.ICGtesting.com
Printed in the USA
BVOW06s0622120815

412948BV00010B/94/P